3X 4/00✓11/01
10X 10/08✓ 1/10 last copy

the baby and fly pie

ALSO BY MELVIN BURGESS:

An Angel for May

Burning Issy

The Cry of the Wolf

THE *baby* AND *fly pie*

MELVIN BURGESS

Simon & Schuster Books for Young Readers

SIMON & SCHUSTER BOOKS FOR YOUNG READERS

An imprint of Simon & Schuster Children's Publishing Division

1230 Avenue of the Americas, New York, NY 10020

Copyright © 1993 by Melvin Burgess

Originally published in Great Britain in 1993 by Andersen Press Limited.

First American Edition, 1996. All rights reserved including the right of reproduction in whole or in part in any form. SIMON & SCHUSTER BOOKS FOR YOUNG READERS is a trademark of Simon & Schuster.

Book design by Paul Zakris. The text for this book is set in 10 point Latin 725.

Printed and bound in the United States of America

First Edition

10 9 8 7 6 5 4 3 2 1

LIBRARY OF CONGRESS CATALOGING-IN-PUBLICATION DATA

Burgess, Melvin.

The baby and Fly Pie / Melvin Burgess. — 1st American ed.

   p.   cm.

   "Originally published in Great Britain in 1993, by Anderson Press"—T.p. verso.

   Summary: In a London of the future, three homeless teens stumble upon a kidnapped baby and hope to be able to exchange her for money to improve their lives.

   ISBN 0-689-80489-X

   [1. Homeless children—Fiction. 2. Babies—Fiction. 3. Kidnapping—Fiction. 4. London (England)—Fiction.] I. Title.

PZ7.B9166Bab 1996

[Fic]—dc20 95-44496

to everyone who has no home

one

It began with a truckload of fish. It was a Tuesday afternoon—Whitechapel, so the fish shouldn't have been there at
all. The truck came lumbering up and we were just closing in
when it upped and tipped—tons and tons of fish, slithering silver under the clouds. We all stared like dummies and then the
stink hit us. We started choking and hit the ground. We hid our
faces and tried not to breathe with our noses but you could
taste it in your mouth, the smell was that bad!

Then the gulls came. I think every gull on Farthing Down
must have seen it or smelled it, and they all told one another
the way they do—by screaming their heads off. Down they
came, screeching and yelling and fighting, even though there
was enough for everyone. It was stink and racket and the gulls
whizzing just past us—we all held our heads and ran like rats.
Mother's Big Boys, Duck and Shiner, started chasing kids and
yelling at them to get back to it, but it was all show; they were
running faster than anyone.

No one was too bothered on Tuesdays. Not much good

comes out of Whitechapel. There's a market there; you can get a box of bruised fruit or stale rolls to eat, but as far as Mother Shelly's concerned there's not much worth selling on. That's why the Big Boys weren't worried. On days like that they just find themselves a quiet place and smoke and talk while the rest of us work. So when someone came along and dumped all that stinking fish right next to us, well . . .

"You better be back for counting," yelled Shiner, still running. He kept running right off the rubbish and he didn't stop until he reached the derelict houses at the edge of the Tip. Then he stuck his hands in his pockets and strolled off. We had an afternoon free.

We're the rubbish kids, Mother's boys and girls. Every day we went out onto the Tip to sort through the rubbish for Mother Shelly—all the metal here, all the furniture there, all the wood and all the paper in separate heaps for her to sell on as salvage. The Tips gave the Mothers a good living, but we were always hungry. We didn't complain. We were orphans and losers and if it wasn't for Mother we'd be on the street. Some kids thought it was a laugh to run wild but they were the ones with someone to go back to when they needed them, the part-timers. We'd have been proper street kids, the real thing, the ones who say, "My mother is the street, my father shoots." What they mean is there are only two things interested in them—the street, and the Death Squads.

That's another thing about the Tips—no one tries to kill you.

Me and my sister Jane used to be street kids before she got us out. On the street you have to beg and steal for pennies. Street kids sleep in shop doorways or in subways and during the day they drift about like litter. You see them everywhere, skinny and ill and dirty and cold, cluttering the place up. Street kids are rubbish—real rubbish, not like Tip rubbish because that's useful.

When the streets get too messy they clean them up. They take you away and no one ever sees you go. People pretend that they take you to nice villages and towns where you have a proper life but we know better than that. The kids see everything.

It's the only thing to do. You can understand their point of view. Better to get rid of us now with a bullet in the head when we're small than wait till we grow up and become proper criminals. Sometimes the big stores and businesses pay for the cleanup. Sometimes, when the kids start pestering the tourists, the council pays. Everyone knows. No one complains. On the Tips we were safe because the Mothers pay to have their kids left alone, but sometimes one of us would disappear on a trip into town. Then Mother would say, "See? You stay out of town and do as Mother tells you," and she'd think it was a good warning to us all.

The trucks from the West End were the best. The trucks from the North were good, too. You could find good clothes— you could keep them if they fitted you and they weren't too good. You could find a bicycle or a watch or a good pair of shoes. But in the trucks from the West End, you could find treasure.

The first thing to look for is food, of course. Sometimes as a bag hits the ground it bursts open—and out come tumbling chops and steaks and fried potatoes and chicken halves. Everyone screams in delight then, because that means the truck's been around the restaurants. You know, the people who go in those restaurants are the richest in the world. They go in just to pass the time, like a kid might play tick-tack-toe or sit in a box when there's not much going on. They sit down and they order steaks or a piece of chicken or half a duck, and potatoes and salad and mushrooms and everything, even though they're not even a bit hungry. And they sit there talking and they eat nothing at all sometimes—maybe just a mouthful of lettuce or a few peas.

Then it all gets cleared away and put in a black garbage bag round the back. And if we're lucky the garbagemen come before the beggars and tramps, and it gets put in the truck and it comes here to us. Sometimes it's still warm.

You have to be quick. The Big Boys have eyes everywhere, they'll take it away if you find something too good. They'll say they're going to take it back for meal time, but they just hide it away and eat it when they're on their own. But sometimes a restaurant has thrown out so much food there's enough for everyone and then we have a wonderful party, sitting on the Tip in old armchairs or settees. Or we get up an old table and put a cloth on it just as if we're proper people who live in a house. And we eat ourselves silly!

"Would sir like another steak?" Mike calls out. He likes to play waiter because waiters work with food all day.

"I think I could manage a small one—no, not that small— or perhaps two," I'll say. And if there's enough, I'll get them.

See? It's not all bad being a rubbish kid. When those West End trucks came, it was like Heaven. You remembered all the stories—the one about the man in Soho Square who throws a wallet full of money in his trash can every morning, just for the kids on the Tip. Or the jeweler so rich he throws out all his old jewels twice a year to make way for the new stuff. A long time ago I used to think the stories were true. My sister Jane said the Mothers make them up to keep us sharp. Whoever makes them up, only the tiniest kids really believe them. If you asked anyone else, "Is it true?" they'd laugh at you for even wondering.

But when the truck comes, then you believe. Even the biggest kids believe everything, anything. There's that wonderful moment when the truck tips. It humps up its back and pours out its treasure—oh, boxes and clothes and mysterious black bags—you name it. And then the kids are there, even before it stops, jumping and crawling, digging and grabbing; and the big kids in charge, Duck and Shiner, start shouting orders and trying to look everywhere at once.

I found treasure once. It was a ring with diamonds in it. The diamonds were tiny but they were real. They cut glass, which everyone knows is a good test for diamonds. Actually, they were quite big for diamonds but I only found that out later on.

I found the treasure in a little cloth bag. I just put my hand in and felt it and I knew at once. I took it out, I had a quick look to see if it really was treasure and then I put it straight in my pocket. I didn't tell. I went on going through the rubbish and I never said a word. Later, when I was on my own, I had a good look at it. You find bits of jewelry quite often and most of it isn't worth much, but I scratched the window at the back of an old warehouse with this ring and then I knew it was real.

I kept the ring in my pocket for a few days while I wandered about the dealers, the antique shops, the jewelers, comparing prices. I was planning on selling it and setting up for myself— me and Jane together. Or I was going to give it to my friend Luke Barker to buy me out and take me on as his boy. Or else I was going to buy a big house and live by the sea. I had all sorts of plans! Just to have it in my pocket made me feel different, special—someone important. It was worth it just for that.

But in my heart I knew what was what. In the end Mother Shelly got to hear I'd been hanging around the jewelers and wanted to know what I was up to, so I gave her the ring, like I always knew I would.

Treasure isn't for rubbish kids, you see. It's too much. Really it just wastes a kid's time. If you were sensible you'd chuck it away if you found some treasure because it just spells trouble, but I don't think anyone could be that sensible.

Our Mother was Mother Shelly. Mother Shelly's kids get the trucks from the West End and the other rich places like Finchley, Richmond and Kensington every week. Everyone knows Mother Shelly's kids wear good clothes and know how to keep warm in the winter. Some of the other Mothers look after their kids better, though. Mother Jennie's kids get proper beds and something hot to eat before they go to sleep. She cooks for them with her own hands. We had to get our own food and Mother Shelly never let us cook inside in case we set fire to the building. We cooked out on the Tip sometimes, but mostly we ate cold.

Our home was a big old office at the edge of the Tips—all black glass and broken windows. It was cold. There were over a hundred of us—Mother Shelly's kids, all bedded down on heaps of old blankets in the open plan office on the fourth floor. Mother's Big Boys and Girls have the third floor and Mother has the two bottom floors all to herself. Some people say it's not fair, but if you get nothing for making good what's the point? On the other floors, the twenty-six floors above us, the pigeons and jackdaws and land gulls nest.

Mother used to say we were lucky to get West End rubbish once a week. Why should she waste her money and time getting us hot meals? Mother Jennie's kids have to have the East End rubbish all the time and we looked down on them. I'd chuck a brick at a Jennie kid if I saw him on our patch and call him an East Ender. But he got a hot meal every day of the year, and there were times when I'd swap half a cold chicken on a wet day in winter for a bowl of hot soup and a proper bed in Mother Jennie's warehouse.

West End rubbish or Whitechapel rubbish, sorting is hard work. If we didn't have enough at the end of the day Mother took it out on Duck and Shiner and they took it out on us. So on this particular Tuesday, the Tuesday of the rotten fish, we were all as pleased as if we'd done something clever to get the afternoon all to ourselves.

Kids were wandering off—to go and sell things they'd stolen from the Tip (all of the rubbish belonged to Mother; she'd bought it) or to spend their pennies on sweets or little things in the market, or to get a few hours in a TV stand. The rest of us moved on along the dump, over to stuff from a day or two ago, or toward the commercial site where it didn't stink and no one was going to bother us.

The Tip was as good a place to spend your day as any if you didn't have to work. There was a big tangle of girders where we liked to hang around. It used to be an old building but it got stripped right down until all that was left were its steel bones. People tried to take them away, too, but it was too much trouble so in the end it all got bulldozed up into a big tangle and left—for us to play on.

We didn't let any of the other kids play there—the Mother Jennie kids or the Mother Anne kids or especially the Mother Malone kids. We had battles there. It was our castle, our palace. I've seen kids pouring blood from a hit with a stone and

Shiraz got knocked out once. It took him ten minutes to come around and we all thought he was dead. That was Phillip Malone who got Shiraz. He was a big strong kid and he could have got to be a Big Boy, but he wasn't fair. He was always picking on the black kids. Shiraz got even, though. He and some others caught Phil on his own one day. They put a rope under his arms and hung him out of a tenth-floor window in one of the old office buildings. I don't how long he was up there, but he couldn't speak by the time we got him down and he'd been sick all down his front. All our kids booed and jeered while we were hauling him back up to the window. They called him the Dangler after that and threatened to tell Shiraz whenever he tried anything. He got sold on to a fertilizer factory in Croydon in the end, and the inside of his mouth turned blue. I used to see him for a while, and then he disappeared.

We climbed and chased around, girls and boys, all together, until it was dinner time. Kids pulled out bits of rubbish they'd found that morning. The ones that had nothing began to wander off back to the Tip or onto the street to beg. I had a chicken leg.

My friend Sham whispered, "Let's explore."

I nodded. I pulled the meat off the chicken leg with my teeth as we walked away across the crushed rubbish underfoot.

"Give us the rest of that leg," he asked, but I shook my head. You never got anything back from Sham.

We called him Sly Sham. We all looked up to him. I was proud to be his friend. We did things if he asked us to and he made us feel ashamed if we said no. Sham was a pickpocket and a thief and a daredevil. He could steal whatever he wanted. He even crept in and stole things from Mother. Once, he took a ride on the roof of a subway train all the way from Kennington to the Angel for a bet. I climbed up to see where he'd drawn his mark, a dagger without a handle, on the roof of the train.

Mother Shelly was always saying what a bad boy he was and how we ought to stay away from him and not be like him, but it was just words. She didn't want too many like him around but one day Sham could be a Big Boy and make good if he played his cards right. The only thing was, you couldn't trust him. He'd been friends with all the others—with Mike and then Tamsin and then Yo-Bo and Kim and Iska and Ben. He did everything with them and went everywhere with them for a few months—and then he dropped them. They'd come up and he'd make a face and walk off, and from then on he treated them as if they stank and he couldn't bear to be near them. Kim was really upset about it. She gets very attached to her friends. She followed him about crying, "What's the matter, Sham? What've I done?" She hadn't done anything, of course. She followed him about for days but he hardly ever spoke to her again.

Now he was my friend. He treated me like I was the only person in the world. I was his lookout when he went thieving. I was as proud as if I were Sham myself, and I never even thought that one day he'd turn around and treat me like dirt.

Sham and I walked off along the edge of the Tip, across the wastes of concrete and long grass, past the garages that no one uses any more, past the warehouses that don't store things any more—toward the commercial Tip at the other end.

The Tip is a city, a city for rats and cats and gulls and kids. There are buildings on it and in it—houses caught up in the spread of the Tip, old warehouses or offices from the boom days, falling to pieces. The gulls roost there at night and in the spring they nest in the windows of the old offices. We climb up and steal the eggs to eat.

When you say you're a rubbish kid people laugh and hold their noses and pretend it's all awful, but the Tip's been good to me. It's fed me, clothed me, given me blankets to sleep on, toys to play with. All for free. Just because someone else had them before, why should that bother the kids? Why should it bother anyone?

The commercial site is supposed to be out of bounds, but no one stops the kids from going where they want on the Tip. Trucks come with loads of rubble, or bicycle tires or old shelving or rotten old fence posts or whatever. They dump it there and the salvage men come—the paper salvage, the wood salvage, the scrap men—the ones the Mothers sell to. You never know what might turn up in the commercial quarter. Those fish should have gone there. Someone had paid the garbagemen to take it to the domestic Tip because it cost less that way.

Today, it was cardboard boxes.

We came around the side of a broken warehouse and there they were, thousands of them. They were heaped up on top of one another so high they'd started spilling through the warehouse windows on the second floor. They weren't flat and in bundles like you usually find them. They were proper, made-up cardboard boxes, all brand-new and unused.

"Someone went bankrupt," said Sham.

"There must've been loads of trucks," I said. They were bashed about and a bit damp from being out for a night, but otherwise they were fine. Some of them had blown off and were floating around the yard; some were on their way out toward the road as if they were heading off to see the world.

Sham and I ran up the stairs in the warehouse to a loading door high in the wall.

I dared him, "Jump!" The boxes were piled up under us, but it was a big drop down.

"You jump," said Sham. We both wanted to. There were seven yards deep of boxes underneath us.

"Cardboard can't hurt you," he said.

"Go on then."

Sham gave me a push. I squealed and hugged the door-frame. Then he went. He leapt out with his arms up and he screamed as he went down, and my heart went down with him. He hit the boxes with a sort of crumpled boom and van-ished. I could hear him thrashing about inside.

"It's hot," he shouted in a muffled voice. "It's hot in here!"

He sounded okay. I stared down, daring myself. It was an awfully long way. Then I went. I went down like a stone, down, down, down—then *bang!* I was sure I'd broken something. *BOOM—crrrrr-ump* went the boxes. They were hard, but they gave. Everything went dim as I went under.

Like Sham said, it was hot, or at least warm down there. I started fighting my way down—swimming and crawling and climbing at the same time, smashing up as many boxes as I could to get there. It got cool as you got further away from the sun. It took ages to get out into the light again. Then we ran back up to do it again.

We did it over and over. After the fourth or fifth time I was exhausted. I'd punched and kicked my way to the ground and I'd come to the warm layer near the sunlight, and I stopped. It was warm and still. The cars on the road a couple of hundred yards off, the gulls still squabbling over the fish, the wind rattling the boxes—it all seemed to belong to another world. You felt that you could lie there forever watch-ing the pale edges of light that crept in, listening to the world outside.

I thought I might just go to sleep. I listened to Sham

punching his way through. He was close. He was making a racket. He got so close I thought he'd fall onto me.

Then he stopped too.

I said, "Sham," quietly.

He said right next to me, "It's only my friend."

There was someone there. I shut up.

"Come here, Fly," said Sham. He was very near, only a couple of boxes away. I kept still. This is where my story starts. He pushed against the boxes; they fell away and the light came in. Sham beckoned. I was ready to run, but he said, "You better come, Fly."

I went.

It was a man. He'd built a little shelter in there. He was lying all crooked. He had one hand wrapped round his side and his side was black with old blood and red with fresh blood. In the other hand he had a gun which was quivering as it pointed at us. It looked as if it could go off in his hand.

"You come in here," he hissed. He sounded terrible. We did as we were told.

His face was dead white; his eyes were too big and too bright. He looked used and worn out although he was only young. He had a bit of beard, he was dressed in good clothes but they were filthy. He was holding a thick blanket to his side and the blanket was red with blood. He'd crushed up some cardboard boxes and he was lying on them, and they were red underneath him, too. It smelled bad.

He was staring at us with those big, too-bright eyes and he looked so terrible. I was staring at him and then at the gun and I couldn't say a word, but Sham said in a quiet voice, "It's all right, we won't do anything."

The man looked at Sham and laughed—as if Sham and I

could do anything! We were just kids. But he looked better then.

That was Sham. When the pressure was on and I just froze up he kept on thinking—as if he were on his own, miles from any trouble, deciding what to have for lunch.

He stared at the man, a long thoughtful look, taking everything in.

"I want you to go shopping for me," said the man.

The gunman made us squat down on the ground with our hands on our heads. He tried to get something out of his anorak pocket and he made the most awful fuss doing it. He was lying almost on his back, trying to keep the gun pointing at our heads while he dug about with his hand and he was whimpering because it hurt him so much. At last he pulled out a big handful of bills. I mean, money. It looked like thousands of pounds. I'd never seen so much money. I felt as though that money was smiling at me—a mean, wicked smile.

He hauled himself up and lay back for a minute, panting with the effort. Then he peeled off a fat little wad and put that in one pile, and then he peeled off a few more which he flung at us.

"That's yours when you get back," he gasped nodding at the fat wad. "I want food, I want medicine—antibiotics and paracetamol or something like that. Painkillers. I want whiskey and I want some milk, a baby's bottle and some diapers."

Sham and I glanced at each other. What did a gangster with a hole in his side want with diapers? He giggled. "Funny, eh?" he snorted, laughing and hurting at the same time. "There's a baby," he added, staring at us. "It needs things— diapers and stuff. Formula and . . . you know."

I didn't know. Mother Shelly picks up babies from time to

the baby and fly pie
13

time and she gets some of her Big Girls looking after them on the second floor. My sister had done it but I'd never even touched a baby.

"You know," insisted the man.

Sham nodded. "I had a baby brother," he said, cool as you like. "Where is it?"

The man nodded at a box by his side. He pushed it over to us with his foot.

Inside the box was a sack. Sham leaned down and opened it up.

The baby was horrible. It was bright red and its brown eyes were all puffy and wet and red. When it saw us it started jerking and twitching and going redder and redder but it couldn't cry because it had a piece of tape stuck over its mouth.

"That's my baby." The gunman smiled. "My little treasure."

Sham reached down to pick it up but he shook his gun and said, "Leave it!" fiercely.

"They need to be held," said Sham. There was a funny moment. The man nodded sharply. Sham reached in and picked it up.

It was twitching and jerking in that horrible way as if it wasn't human at all. It was in a terrible mess—you know what babies are like. It had peed and crapped and that man hadn't done anything for it. It held out its arms and Sham cradled it against his chest. It looked awkward but he seemed to know what he was doing. At last it stopped twitching and began wriggling and nuzzling into Sham, making soft, choked little cries.

"Can I take the tape off?" begged Sham.

The man shook his head. "She cries," he said, watching Sham closely. "When your friend comes back with the stuff you can take the tape off and you can feed it." He nodded at the pile of money. "And you can have that. I mean it," he added. "It's a job. I'll pay you. Just do as I say."

Sham cuddled the baby. It was reaching its arms up to him and making grunting noises. You felt you'd do anything to get that tape off.

"You go," said Sham to me. "And make sure you come back."

two

We call it making good. It's plans and dreams and you can't always tell the difference. Everyone's going to make good but not many do. Sham was. Unlike most of us, he believed it. He boasted about it—even to Mother Shelly and I think she believed it because she used to put him in charge and give him jobs.

My big thing was getting out—out of London, out of England, away to a proper country. You know the sort of place—America, Australia, France—where there's a place for everyone. You get adopted and looked after just by being there! Everyone can make a life for themselves, not just the lucky ones. I wanted to get out and live in one of those countries and have enough money and a big house by the sea.

Why not? People do. Maybe I could rob a bank with Sham. Maybe I'd find treasure. Maybe—but in my heart I knew all that was too much. I wasn't the sort. I'm not special. Jane said that dreams have to be big enough to keep you going and small enough to come true. So I had another dream, a regular dream just big enough to work.

I didn't want to be a rubbish sorter all my life. I didn't want to join a gang or sell seconds like the rest. I wanted to be a baker. Does that sound strange? But a baker has a good life. Everyone needs him, the world passes through his shop. He sells bread to poor people and fancy cakes to rich people. I want to be a baker for all those reasons but mostly I want to be a baker because a baker is always warm and he always has enough to eat. One day, I'll have a shop of my own and have cream slices and Viennese twists in the window. I'll eat them every day—and whatever I can't eat and I can't sell I'll give to the kids who live on the street, like my friend Luke does.

I never talked about it. Sham would have sneered because working hard isn't smart. But Luke wanted me. Not many kids have someone willing to train them, but Luke had a little bakery and no kids of his own and he took a shine to me. The only trouble was, I belonged to Mother Shelly and Mother Shelly doesn't let her kids go for nothing.

Luke's a good man. He doesn't put powder in his bread to make the flour go further. He lets the dough rise all night and that's why his bread is better than anyone else's. It comes with a thick chewy crust and a snappy, crackly surface so good you could eat it all day. If he wanted to, Luke could get a bigger shop in a better place. But—"The more money you make, the more trouble you make," says Luke. To get a shop on the High Street you have to pay big money to the council and big money to the gangs. So Luke keeps his little shop tucked away down a back alley off Laura Street and he sells out by lunch time and takes the afternoon off. He pays a little every week to the Monroe Gang and everyone leaves him alone. It's big enough for Luke. As for me, I'd give anything to have that little shop and get up at five every morning to knead the loaves and put the breakfast buns on to rise.

*   *   *

Making good is just a dream for most of us. But all dreams—big ones and little ones, ones that come true and ones that never can—they're all the same in one way: they all cost money. And as I ran out of the Tip with my pocket full of money, that's how I was thinking. I couldn't see anything except that pile of money the gunman had in his anorak. That pile of money was—dreams!

You could do anything. You were set up! You'd made good. You didn't need to work, you could sail away and buy a house by the sea anywhere in the world. Jane wouldn't like it, of course. She'd have turned up her nose and said, "Bad money." But she was a girl, she only had to look pretty and keep her nose clean and find the right man. She didn't know what was what as far as I was concerned. I felt I'd made good just looking at that money. I thought I'd seen thousands and thousands of pounds.

I didn't stop to wonder what that man was doing bleeding in a heap of rubbish when he had so much. I didn't stop to think about what he was doing to the baby, or whose baby it was or why he had it. I just ran to do the shopping as fast as I could before he and his money disappeared.

Someone shouted at me as I ran off the concrete onto Commercial Road. "Hey, you—kid!" he yelled. They don't like us running past the Depot Office. I ran faster. I had a hundred pounds in my pocket and I was dangerous. I felt people could tell I had it just by looking at me.

Spending money isn't easy. I couldn't go into a supermarket because they don't let kids in there—not rubbish kids, anyway. I had to go around to all the little shops and, of course, everyone wanted to know where I'd got it.

The diapers and formula and stuff wasn't so hard.

"I'm on an errand," I said. You can explain most things like that.

The shop girl shrugged. She didn't care. "Anything else?" she asked. "Baby wipes? Cream, powder?"

"Oh, yeah," I said. I didn't know any of that stuff but I felt that this baby ought to have everything.

When I started paying for cooked meat with a fifty, they all looked at me.

"On an errand," I said.

"Who for, Fly?" asked the man behind the counter.

I said, "Mother Shelly," because she's the only person I know who has money like that. The shopkeeper had a good look at me. Mother Shelly never sent a kid my age on an errand with that sort of money. He'd remember: Fly Pie was spending money on Tuesday afternoon.

It was bad for me and it was bad for the man with the gun. It would have been better for me to catch a bus and go somewhere where I wasn't known but he couldn't wait.

"Half an hour," he'd said, tapping the barrel of his gun.

I had to run to get to the liquor store on Woodplace Lane where Sala will sell booze to anyone. Sala stared hard at me when I asked for cigarettes and three bottles of whiskey.

"On an errand," I said weakly. He shrugged and turned away to get my stuff. He had to go round the back to get the whiskey. That was when I glanced up at the little color TV Sala had behind the counter. The little voice from the TV buzzed away low because it was only for Sala's ears. But the shop was empty and I could just make out a few words.

". . . three dead men . . ." said the tiny voice on the TV. I glanced over the candy counter out of habit. Normally I might have tried to steal something, but not today.

". . . the burnt-out car was found three miles away early

this morning . . ." said the TV. Sala glanced across at me from where he was plonking three bottles of whiskey into a bag. I smiled at him.

". . . kidnapped baby . . ." said the little voice.

I forgot everything. On the TV? It couldn't be! I strained forward to hear more but then Sala came right up and put the bag on the counter. He started counting out my change and I had to try and look as if nothing was happening. I was holding on to the counter to stand still.

". . . received demands for the return of the baby . . . seventeen million pounds . . ." said the announcer. Sala banged the money on the table.

"Only a bad man wants three bottles," he said.

"It's got to last awhile," I explained.

". . . Finchley home . . ." continued the voice. ". . . an extensive police search . . ." Then there was a photograph. It didn't look the same but I knew. The baby on TV was smiling and clean. Ours was ugly and red and dirty and it twitched. But I knew.

". . . the dead men . . ." repeated the TV.

The baby hidden away, covered in piss and shit with a strip of sticky tape over its mouth. Seventeen million pounds . . .

I stared at Sala. My mouth was moving. All I could think was seventeen . . . seventeen million . . .

"What's up with you?" Sala demanded. Then the door opened and two men came in.

"Two hours for a bus from Croydon," one of them was complaining.

I came to. I felt trapped. I turned and sprinted out of the shop.

"Hey!" shouted one of the men. He swiped at me as I pushed past him.

"Hey!" shouted Sala. He must have thought I'd stolen something the way I was going.

"I'd have walked if I had legs like that," remarked the other man as I made it to the pavement. I was really moving. I had seventeen million pounds chasing after me.

Back in his cardboard den, the gunman went straight for the whiskey and paracetamol. I had to open the tops for him. He wouldn't put down his gun. He flung a handful of tablets into his mouth and tipped back the whiskey . . . a big mouthful of it. Then he leaned back and looked at me.

"Thanks," he said.

He didn't seem to care for the food. He just looked at the chicken and fruit I'd bought as if he didn't know what it was for.

I had a big tin of dried baby formula and a bottle of fresh milk. Sham poured the fresh milk into the baby bottle and glanced anxiously at the man. He nodded. Sham tore the strip of tape off the baby's mouth.

The baby gasped. It hurt. She stared at Sham. You could see how filthy she was—her mouth was white and red where the tape had been and the rest of her was nearly black. Then she opened her mouth for the biggest, loudest howl she had ever made. Sham stuck the bottle in.

The milk was cold, just out of the fridge in the shop. But she didn't care. She gargled and glugged for a second, seeing what it was. Then she wrapped her little hands around the bottle, curled up her legs, as if she wanted to wrap her whole self right around the bottle, and sucked and sucked and sucked. . . .

"The first drink we've had all day," said the man, tapping his own bottle. We all sat and watched the baby guzzling. It was very quiet, there was just the wind rattling the boxes outside and the baby going glug, glug, glug. After a bit she opened her eyes and looked at Sham. She let go of the bottle and reached up to play with his fingers.

"Give me some," said the man. Sham handed him the milk and the gunman tipped it down his neck in long swallows . . . he and his baby, both guzzling milk.

After a bit Sham laid the baby on the ground and began to undress her. It stank. He began scraping away at the shit on her bum and she whimpered. The skin was all red and there was blood.

"Must've been that shit . . . sitting in its own shit for two days," said the man, watching. He was surprised.

Sham knew what he was doing. He cleaned the baby up with the wipes and started smearing on cream and stuff. It looked odd because Sham was so cool and smart and there was never anyone but Sham on his mind. But here he was, cleaning up the baby like a little mother.

"I had a baby brother," he explained.

"Did you have a mother?" I asked in surprise.

"I told you . . . I told everyone," said Sham. So he had. But everyone said that, and no one ever believed it.

The gunman began to relax. His head tipped back, he stared at the pale light finding its way through the boxes. He looked fragile, made out of china. I thought that if he relaxed too much he'd never wake up.

I found myself staring at the pile of money. It was all there, lying by his hand.

"You need a doctor," Sham said.

The man turned his bright eyes on him.

"We could get someone," said Sham. "We could get one of Mother's Big Girls—they fix us up all the time when we get hurt."

The man looked down at the ground and made a face as if he didn't care.

"You need someone to help you," said Sham. He finished up with the diaper and started to dress her again. I still couldn't believe he knew how to do that.

"You need us," said Sham.

"Kids," said the man. He sighed. "Just a pair of kids."

"We're all you got," said Sham. "I know about babies. We can do things—get things, make calls for you—get someone to look after you."

I wanted to shout at him, "Shut up!" because the whole thing was too big for us. It was on television! It was seventeen million pounds. What we had to do was get away as soon as we could.

"His sister." Sham nodded at me. "Your sister has done nursing for Mother, hasn't she?" he asked.

"I don't want my sister in this," I said quickly.

"Listen . . ." began Sham, but I wasn't having it.

I said, "Look, mister—I did what you asked me, I got the stuff. Maybe I'll do it again if you like, but how about paying me first?" I nodded at the pile of money. My money.

The man smiled and nodded. He took it up in his hand and held it out to me. "You did a good job," he said. "Take it. There's more," he added. "Enough for everyone . . ."

I reached out. I nearly had it in my hand.

"Don't give him that," said Sham suddenly and the man's hand went back.

I couldn't believe it. It was half his!

"He'll run off and spend it and then they'll want to know where he got it from. The place'll be crawling in half an hour."

"No, I won't!"

Sham began talking quickly to the gunman, glancing at me

out of the corner of his eye. "You need us. We're all you got. You need me and you need him because someone has to look after the baby and someone has to do the errands. You pay him off now and that's it, you'll never see him again. . . ."

"You bastard," I said. But he didn't even look at me.

The gunman smiled. He raised his hand to hush Sham. Then he said to me, "Tell me, kid . . . what you want . . . What do you want most in the whole world?"

My heart started going again. I got cold. I don't know why that frightened me. He was smiling at me as if he was my friend.

"Tell me," he said. "Tell me."

I glanced at Sham. "I got a friend, see . . ."

It all came out. All about Luke and how he kept a little shop and always sold out of bread by lunchtime. I felt stupid. Sham was watching me the whole time.

The gunman nodded. "That's a good thing to want," he said when I'd finished. "How much? How much does it cost to buy a boy from his Mother?"

I shrugged. "Maybe a thousand," I told him.

The man smiled. He patted his pocket. I knew what he was going to say. "I have that much right here," he said. He smiled again. "I have thousands and thousands. You run some errands for me, make a few calls, and I'll give it to you."

I nodded. I could have cried. This treasure wouldn't be easy to get rid of.

"What about me?" demanded Sham. He held the baby on his lap with the bottle still stuck in its mouth and he stared at the gunman intently.

"You can have what you want, too," whispered the man. "You can have everything—both of you. There's enough for everyone."

He was lying full out on the floor. He looked as if he was falling asleep.

"What do we do?" asked Sham eagerly. "Who do we get in touch with?"

The man shook his head.

I looked at the man. He'd closed his eyes. "It's a kidnap," I said. His eyes opened. "I saw it on the TV," I said.

The gunman smiled. "I was on the TV, was I?"

"How much?" said Sham. "The ransom, I mean?"

The man looked at me.

I licked my lips. "Seventeen million," I said. He smiled and watched us to see how we reacted. "That's what the TV said," I said to Sham. He licked his lips.

"Hey—this is the big time," he said.

"You with me?" said the gunman.

Sham nodded.

"Partner," said the man.

"Partner," said Sham.

"I just want enough to buy myself out—get into Luke Barker's shop . . ." I babbled. I wanted it to be clear to every-one—I was just running errands. Sham looked at me in disgust and I couldn't meet his eye. I was a baby.

The man stared at the boxes above his head. "Luke Barker's" he said. "I know it. He makes good bread."

I nodded. "I want to make good bread, too, please." I was trying not to cry.

"Wise kid," said the gunman.

Sham snorted. That money was out of my league but it was right in his. Where did being wise get you? "Little baker's shop," he sniffed.

"You can be our messenger boy. You run the errands, fetch things we need," said the gunman. "First you bring your sister here to fix me up. Tell her. Ask her what she wants. She can have anything. . . ."

"Just pay her," said Sham. "She doesn't need to have whatever she feels like."

"It's important," insisted the gunman, looking up at Sham from down there on the floor. "Everyone gets what they want, whatever they want. We stick together. We pay our way."

"It doesn't cost a grand to buy him out," said Sham, nodding at me. He'd already left me behind.

The gunman shook his head. "Don't try to rob the whole world," he said. "We stick together. See? Everyone gets what they want—anything, everything they want. There's enough. Seventeen million pounds. We stick together. . . ."

"Okay, sure," said Sham, nodding. "I see, of course. It's safer that way."

"There's enough," said the man. "Seventeen million pounds, partner . . ."

Sham smiled. He cuddled the baby. "Partner," he said.

three

I knew right then I shouldn't get my sister involved. Jane was different. She was a good girl, you know the sort. While the rest of us were out having a good time Jane would stay in and wash her clothes or do her hair. She was always trying to learn things—reading and writing or sewing or adding up. She was stupid. Who needs to read and write on a rubbish tip? But she did it anyway, and she kept herself neat and clean and did as she was told. She didn't have big dreams about sailing away and getting rich. She just wanted to marry a man with a job, or get to work in a little shop and end up in a couple of rooms with kids of her own.

I shouldn't talk my sister down. The reason why I was a Mother Shelly kid and not on the streets was all because of her. For a street kid, getting to be a Mother's boy is all you ever dream about. I don't know how Jane managed it, because hundreds try it and never make it. Maybe it's impressive the way she always turns out in a clean dress with her hair brushed and her good manners, even when she's had to walk through the dirt to get there.

When I was small she was like my mother even though she was only a couple of years older than me. I used to think she was a superstar, I used to do everything like she did. I was a baby then. Things change—I grew up. No one was going to marry me because I wore clean clothes and said "thank you" nicely. Don't get me wrong, she was my sister and I was proud of her. If anyone had laid a finger on her I'd have given them a battering. But I didn't like her around. She didn't know the right things. She didn't know how to steal food or pick pockets or pull a fast one. Gangsters and guns—that wasn't Jane. I didn't want her in on it. She'd try to tell us off and I'd be embarrassed. But Sham knew what he was doing. I wanted my share of that money and he'd roped me in whether I wanted it or not.

I was supposed to go straight to get Jane but I didn't. I was hungry, so I lined up with the others for supper. It was stupid, I wasn't thinking. But there's not much thinking gets between a kid and his supper.

We middle kids have our supper at a row of trestle tables outside the office. In the morning, before you feed yourself, you have to find stuff to hand over to the Big Boys for supper that evening. That way everyone gets at least one meal a day. Today we had cabbages and carrots. I don't know where Mother got them from but there were loads of them, spilling out right along the middle of the table. It was raw but there was lots of it.

First we had to stand in front of our places to be counted. Mother counts her kids twice a day. You have to be there.

That's when they found out Sham was missing.

Shiner didn't take long to find out Sham had gone off with me. He was furious. Mother would take it out on him if one of his boys was missing.

"Where's he gone, Fly?"

"I don't know, Shine, I really don't," I whined. I never thought! It was so obvious he'd pick on me. I was terrified because I still had money slipped inside my shoe.

"You better tell," he threatened.

"We went over the commercial. He cleared off. You know what he's like," I begged.

Shiner looked into my face. I just cringed. He scared the juice right out of me. He was a big kid with scars crisscrossed all over his face like someone scribbled on him with a knife. He made those scars by cutting himself and rubbing ash in the wounds—just to show how mean he was. He stared at me in disgust while I cringed and everyone held their breath and watched.

"You get on with it!" he yelled to the other kids, hardly taking his eyes off me. They forgot about me and dived at the tables and began munching carrots and trying to break up the cabbages. That wasn't easy because we had no knives. The best way was to beat them on the floor and jump on them. I felt sick. It wasn't just the trouble. I was missing supper! I hadn't eaten anything since that chicken leg and I was ravenous.

Shiner grabbed my shoulder. "You're going to see Mother," he said grimly.

Mother Shelly was sitting at a desk by the telephone where she sells the stuff we collect or things we make—little animals out of scraps of soap, or pretty stars out of silver paper. She was a big woman dressed in leather trousers and a leather jacket. You never saw her any other way. She had straight blond hair and long crooked teeth. She was fat but she was as strong as a man and even the biggest boys were frightened of her.

"One missing, Mother," Shiner said. "Sly Sham." He gave me a shake. "He was with him last."

Mother Shelly looked at me. "The baker," she said. She remembered everyone. "Fly Pie."

She gave me that name. When I had time off, Luke used to let me in the bakery to practice. Luke said I have cold hands and I work quickly, and that's why I'm such a good pastry cook. He has warm hands so we plan how when we finally get together, he's going to make the bread and Danish pastries and all the yeasty things, and I'll be the pastry cook.

Sometimes I used to take things to Mother to try and get in her good books. Once, I made her a chocolate pie. Luke showed me how. It was difficult—fancy flaky pastry made with ground almonds and a thick chocolate cream inside. I was so proud! It was the most wonderful thing you ever saw and I'd made it.

When I gave it to Mother she was impressed, too. She almost snatched it off me. It looked so good. She took a huge bite and I watched her eyes smiling at me over the top of it as she swilled it round in her mouth. She nodded at me; she was really pleased. I thought she'd let me go just because it tasted so good!

But then her face changed. She opened her mouth and stuck out her tongue and there was something fat and black on the end of it. I could see her eyes crossing to try and see what it was.

I don't know how a fly got in the chocolate—I was stirring it for ages to make sure it didn't burn and I never saw it. But there it was—a big, fat bluebottle.

"Flies!" she roared, spitting pie out across the room. I'd have eaten that pie even if it was full of flies—we never get chocolate. But Mother was disgusted.

"Bloody fly pie," she bawled. She chucked the pie at me across the room and I ran for it. Everyone was hooting. She wouldn't take anything off me for ages after that, but the name stuck: Fly Pie—Fly for short.

Mother didn't ask me straight off. She looked at me and she said, "I have a letter from Luke Barker. He says, if he can't pay me money he'll give me free bread and cakes."

I nodded miserably.

"Luke Barker makes good bread," she observed. She leaned forward. "Tell Mother what you know, Fly—tell her everything."

"I don't know, honest, I don't know," I gurgled.

I should have told her! I was so stupid that day! She'd have let me go to Luke. I know she'd have let me go—but I just wasn't ready to give up my treasure; not so soon.

She looked disgusted. "He knows something," she said to Shiner.

"It's not that—I'm a coward, that's all. Ask anyone . . ."

Shiner snorted. "That's true," he said.

Mother laughed. "Not much good for anything but a baker, then," she said. "Listen, Fly Pie—you tell me what you know or I'll sell you to the sewer men."

"Mother, but I don't, I don't . . . He just went off on his own. . . ."

"Where did he say he was going?"

"He said . . . he said he had a deal. He wanted me to come in on it, but . . ."

"But what?"

"It was the Marley lot," I muttered.

"Ah!"

Mother Shelly and Mother Marley were always fighting. They were always trying to poach on each other's territory or get kids off each other. Mother was hard to fool, but she was always willing to believe that Mother Marley was after her kids.

"So that's it—he's been set up, the little idiot," she snapped at Shiner. "Why can't you keep your eyes open?"

Shiner gave me a nasty look. "Sorry, Mother," he muttered.

"Get round there now," ordered Mother. "Tell her I want my boy back. You can go back to your supper," she told me. "And next time tell Shiner!" she bellowed at me. She swung at me and I ducked and went running. I could hear her behind me bawling at Shiner as I ran out of the building.

I'd really messed it up. I knew I'd messed it up even while I was doing it. I'd wanted to hold on to my secret and believe for a few hours that I was going to be someone big. I'd lied to her and she'd find out and now she'd never give me to Luke.

I didn't go for supper. Shiner would only come to give me a battering anyway. I had to hurry if I was going to get anything out of this—it wouldn't take them long to find out I was lying. I ran straight around behind the office and went to look for Jane.

Jane was fourteen, ready for selling on. Street kids cost nothing, of course, but people are willing to pay for kids who will do as they're told. Mostly, the girls get sold on to brothels or factories where no one wants to go, but we were all sure Jane was going to be one of the lucky ones. She could have served in a shop or looked after babies or anything—because you could trust her, you see. Right now she'd be on the third floor.

You sneak up the back stairs. You can see into the kitchen through the service door. Behind the kitchen is the place where the Big Girls sleep, and kids like to spy there, too—to see the girls undressing.

I had a good ogle—at the food, not at the girls. Right next to me there was a girl I knew—Daffy, we called her, because she had a squeaky voice. She was cutting up vegetables and arranging them in a big salad bowl. There was everything. Red peppers and yellow peppers and green peppers, and onions and lettuces and tomatoes all wet and fresh and clean. I just stared. I was so hungry I even forgot the trouble I was in.

Then she spotted me.

"You—get out of here," she snapped, waving her little knife at me. But not so loud that anyone else could hear.

"Daffy, wait," I hissed. "I've got to find Jane."

Daffy cocked her head and frowned. "What do you want her for?" she asked, glancing over her shoulders. She began chopping up a bright yellow pepper. "She's not here, forget it," she quacked.

I groaned out loud. I couldn't believe it—Jane was always in, she never went anywhere. And then just when I need her she disappears! "Where's she gone?" I begged.

"What's up with you?"

"Please, Daffy!"

"Don't you worry about her. Leave it till tomorrow," she advised. She glared at me. "Go on, clear off. You're asking for trouble, Fly Pie."

"I've got to find her," I insisted.

One of the other girls came across. I ducked down but she saw me.

"He's looking for his sister," explained Daffy in a flat voice. "Janey. You know . . ."

The other girl sniggered. I poked my head back up. "I've got to find her—it's important," I pleaded.

"I don't think she likes little boys anymore," sneered the girl. She giggled.

I stared at her. Daffy gave me a funny look. "Is it that important, Fly?" she asked.

"Yeah, really . . ."

"Try Coulsdon—the High Street," she said, not looking at me. "Be careful, though."

"What's she doing there?"

The other girl snorted in amusement. Daffy shrugged. "There's a street fair there tonight, don't ask me," she muttered, chopping away at her pepper. She flung a handful into the salad bowl. "Scram, Fly Pie," she squeaked, suddenly angry. I turned and started down the stairs.

"Better take some money with you," jeered the other girl. I didn't think what she meant at the time. I was too full of the other thing.

It was six o'clock—rush hour. The traffic jams last for hours. You can see the smog the cars make when you look in toward town and when the wind blows out, you can see the murky air rolling up the street and over the rooftops. Out here on the edge of town the traffic wasn't so bad but it was still almost as quick to walk. Even so I caught the bus. The bus is a treat. You ride up there above all the fumes and stink; you can see things in a different way from up high on a double-decker.

The driver watched me dig out my pennies and he rattled the money in the tray by his seat to make sure it was real before he gave me a ticket. I climbed up to the top and got a window seat.

"Traveling in style today?" It was an old man with very black skin and pale gray hair in the seat behind me. He grinned at me and I grinned back. "Wicked!" he said, and he winked. "What did you find, the Crown Jewels?"

"Pair of shoes—real leather," I told him. I was nervous. I had thirty pounds stuffed in my shoe for medicines and bandages and so on, and that money wanted to draw attention to me. The old man nodded and smiled. "I got twenty for 'em," I lied.

"That's a good price," said the old man. He had a big brown paper packet in his arms and he squeezed it, so it crackled gently.

"You got ripped off," said a woman across the passage. "You can't get decent leather shoes for under a hundred quid, not even second-hand."

"Don't spoil his day for him," scolded the old man. "He's made a killing—he's riding the bus!"

I smiled again and pressed my nose against the window. I could see right down along Coulsdon Road, into the dirty brown air ahead.

Now I had time to think. I had time to think how stupid I'd been! Lining up there for my chunk of raw cabbage and a moldy black carrot! Sham wouldn't have done that; he'd have been in and out of there like a ghost and no one would have known. And telling that stupid lie to Mother! My mouth had just gone blabbing on. Mother could have done things with the information I had, she could have made some real money for herself and then she'd have given me to Luke for sure. Now someone else would get the credit for telling her and I was just another lying kid who didn't know what was good for him.

I could still make it right. The bus went right past Luke's shop. All I had to do was jump off and run round the back and tell him everything. He'd be making up the dough to stand overnight. Maybe he'd come round with me and help me tell Mother Shelly.

"The boy was frightened—it's big business!" he'd say. "There was a gun!" he'd say. I could hear him saying it, with his hand on my shoulder, looking after me and doing what was best.

I felt even sicker when I thought that, because I knew I wasn't going to do it. Isn't that strange? But that's treasure for you. Treasure is dreams and even when you know you should, you can't let dreams go. That's how life goes on from day to day.

I felt sick on the way, with the bus coughing its way up the road like an old man. I felt sick while it stopped in a traffic jam for five whole minutes right opposite Luke's road. I stared down at the little alley where his shop was tucked away and I knew I could get there in less than a minute if I ran. But the bus started up again and I felt the shop disappearing into the traffic behind me and I felt sicker than ever.

I thought about that gunman, too. He wasn't rich. He was wearing good clothes, but you can always tell a poor man even if he makes money because he's small and his skin and his teeth are bad and he has a sort of pinched look about him. He'd been breathing the bad city air all his life. Like me, I don't suppose he'd ever seen the sea. In London you're lucky to see the sky.

Maybe he'd been a Mother's boy. Maybe he'd been bought up by some gang and ended up running errands and getting nowhere. Now he was trying for himself—trying to make good. He'd found his treasure and he'd kept it and now he was bleeding to death among the rubbish with no one to help him but a pair of kids.

We went sailing down Coulsdon Road, past the cars growling and honking, past the shops and the people crowding and running and working and stealing and fighting—past the street kids tugging at people's coats asking for money, the rich people in their big cars with dark glass, the shopkeepers, the men lounging about.

I thought of all the things you could do with seventeen million pounds. . . .

I heard the fair before I saw it. Everyone started peering out of the windows and smiling. That's how a fair makes you feel. Then the music went loud and there it was down a side road—a solid mass of people and smoke and stalls and sound. I jumped off the bus and ran down into the hot crowd.

It was so noisy! I was spinning around and around, trying to see all the good things for sale, and if I could steal anything, and where my friends were and where my sister was all at the same time. A boy I knew came up to me and pushed a bright mass of cotton candy in my face.

"Sticky Fly Pie!" he shouted gleefully. I just gobbled away and he watched me for a second before he took it back.

"Seen my sister?" I shouted. He shrugged. Then his friends swept him along and he disappeared—gone in a second into the crowd. I could see his cotton candy jogging about in the air over people's heads so it wouldn't get crushed.

That cotton candy brought my hunger back. I was slavering. I bought myself a hot dog and pushed my way through scarfing it—past a stall selling jewelry, past a man standing in a puddle shouting about God—he was drunk, or mad, or both or something. My eyes were popping out of my head. It was impossible to find anything in that pack!

Finally someone told me they'd seen Jane by a reggae band. I was getting really cross with her. She hated all that! She was so stubborn it was impossible to get her to do what she didn't want to—and here she was in the worst place to find someone, just where she never went.

I soon found the band—you couldn't miss it. They have these enormous speakers, big as front doors, all piled on top of one another going boom, boom, boom so loud it knocks the breath out of you. I kept missing her because she was dressed up. She had a floppy hat on and a new dress. It wasn't her sort of dress at all, all short and thin and I saw her a few times before I realized who it was. I went running after her but she was right up by the speakers where the music was loudest and the crowd thickest, and I had to fight to get to her. She couldn't even dance in that pack and the music was deafening. Jane used to say it's only so loud so you can't make out the mistakes. When I caught up she was staring hard at the band as if nothing else mattered.

I tugged her shoulder. "Jane!" I shouted, but she couldn't hear. She just ignored me and tried to edge away. I had to pull and tug before she turned around and glared at me.

"Oh," went her mouth when she saw who it was. "It's you . . ." she mouthed.

I tried to pull her away, but she didn't want to come. I almost had to drag her. She was looking up and around as if someone was after her. I dragged her around behind the band.

"Davey," she said, straightening her hat. She never calls me Fly Pie. "Oh, Davey, my poor ears! I think I'm going deaf—everything's humming!" She pulled her hat down over her ears and made a face.

"What were you doing up there?" I demanded. But she shrugged and shook her head.

"Wanted to see what I was missing?" she suggested, and she laughed again, crookedly, shaking her head as if she could shake out the ringing in her ears.

"Listen," I said.

* * *

It was the right place to tell a secret, behind the stage in among all the electrics. There was so much noise I could hardly hear myself. She looked curiously at me as I told.

When I'd finished she grabbed my arm and pulled me out, away from the fair. That was the wrong way and I tried to pull back but she wasn't having it, so we had to double back afterward. I thought she'd had enough of all those people. She was running, she dragged me all the way. Once we'd left the noise she started asking me questions—how ill was the man, was the baby okay, how much money did he have? And she kept asking me about what he'd said—about there being enough for everyone, about sticking together and paying properly, because for once, there was enough money for everyone.

"Davey," she said. "Davey . . ." She grabbed hold of my arm. She looked at me as if she could fill me up with something—I don't know what. She was about to say something but she changed her mind and shook her head.

"We'll need bandages," she said.

"I've got money—lots of it—it's in my shoe," I told her proudly.

We found a drugstore on the High Street. Jane came out with a big bag and we caught the bus back to Farthing Down.

On the bus, sitting side by side on the top, Jane took my hand and smiled at me. She had a bag of little colored lollipops she'd bought at the drugstore. "Remember?" she said.

I remembered. She used to take me on a bus ride for my birthday. We didn't go anywhere. The ride was enough for us. As we rode we'd eat our way through a bag of those bright little lollipops. We were very proud to have birthdays because most of the other kids didn't have them. They didn't have a family either, but we did. Actually, both the family and the birthdays weren't real ones. Jane just picked a couple of days for us and we celebrated them every year, and that's why we went on those bus rides years ago and felt special—somehow made for better things than the rest of them. We used to ride along like rich kids and Jane would tell me stories about when we still lived at home and had everything.

When I was little and Jane used to look after me she always used to make me behave by saying, "What would Mum and Dad say if they saw you do that?" It nearly always worked. The thing was, all the other kids belonged on the Tip. They'd been dumped by their mothers because there wasn't enough money to feed them, but me and Jane, we were just lost. Our mum and dad had lost us years ago by accident. They were very unhappy about it and they were always out looking for us. One day, they'd find us. They might just walk past us in the street and recognize us, or come into the dorm at Mother Shelly's to find us. And everything would be all right again! Sometimes on those birthday bus rides one of us would point out of the window at some rich woman walking down the street with a servant walking after her carrying her shopping bags, and we'd say, "Do you think that's Mum?" and the other would look and make a face and say, "Nah! Not rich enough," or, "Too ugly!"

Jane could remember Mum and Dad. They were rich! Dad worked in a big business and Mum stayed at home all day just so she could look after us. We all lived together in a big house and we went to nursery school and had proper dinners at the table, and we would have gone to school, too, if we hadn't got lost.

It happens. Kids get lost every day in London. You can see people walking around with even quite big kids tied to their wrists so they can't get separated. It happened to us on the subway. It was a special surprise trip. It might have been a trip to the zoo, or to a big restaurant, or to the cinema. But we never found out because a big crowd got onto the train and we got separated, and when we tried to follow Mum and Dad off the train, we found we were following the wrong people. We got lost. It's easy to get lost in London, because London's the biggest place in the world.

Well, it was just a game, you understand? Real life's not like that. In real life Jane couldn't even remember what our last names were. She was only four when we went on the street. She remembered a big woman with a limp who used to look after us. The police came for her one day. We hid and then ran away. Maybe it would have been better if we'd hung around with the neighbors or someone but after we'd run for it we couldn't find our way back and that was that. We weren't even sure if that woman was our mother—she could have been an aunt or our grandmother or anyone, really. But those other stories made us both feel good and even though I hadn't believed them for years, I liked to pretend every now and then that maybe it was true after all.

We sat together now on the top deck next to one another. It felt good. We held hands and sucked our lollipops and for a little while it felt just like it used to, and this was another special day for two important people. On my birthday, Jane always used to say to me, "What do you want for your birthday, Davey?" And I'd invent some wonderful, impossible thing and she'd promise that I'd have it.

She didn't ask me anything like that this time. There was a sense that everything we wanted was ours already—almost. We were on our way to make good. I was so relieved that she'd come along with me! Knowing Jane, I'd thought she might refuse to go or insist on telling Mother or the police. We smiled at each other. Her face was bright. She looked so bright I wondered if she was all right. I thought she was going to tell me something but she didn't.

The bus snorted and jerked on its way to the Tip. I tried not to think about what would happen next.

four

It wasn't easy getting Jane into the commercial site. It's one thing for a rubbish kid to slip by, but what's a pretty girl in her best dress and high heels doing on the Tip? She slipped off her shoes and ran when I gave her the all clear and we hurried around to the mountain of boxes. I wasn't sure where the hideout was. I started whispering, "Sham? Sham . . ."

He came out white and fearful.

"I thought you weren't coming," he whined. He rubbed his eyes and looked at Jane sulkily. He said, "We don't need her anymore."

I ducked down and pushed my way into the den. The baby was lying in her box. The tape was back on—there was a big roll of tape in the box with her and she was playing with it. Her eyes followed me. The man lay there very still. His eyelids were half shut but you could see his eyes. They were gray and still. I stared, waiting for the eyes to flicker.

"I've been in there with him," said Sham. He sounded

close to tears. I pushed a box down on top of the man. He didn't even twitch. The gunman was dead.

Jane followed me in. She glanced at the man, then at the baby. "Oh, look, poor little thing," she whispered. "Who's put that tape on its face?" She picked it up and at once the baby began to struggle and jerk and grunt.

"It screams when you take it off," warned Sham.

Jane cuddled the baby to her and stroked its head.

"Poor little thing," murmured Jane. "Poor little thing."

We watched her nursing the baby for a while. She sang a lullaby. I heard Sham snort. Three kids and a dead man in a rubbish tip, and there she was singing a lullaby!

"Rock a bye baby, on the tree top . . ." she sang, just as if she was in a real bedroom putting the baby to sleep.

"Do you want to come in on this?" Sham interrupted.

Jane stopped singing, but she didn't look up.

"This is the big time," said Sham. "That man told me everything. It's ransom. There's just us—us three. All the kidnappers are dead. He was the last one. I'm his partner. He gave me that baby. It's mine."

Jane stroked the baby's face. She didn't say anything.

"You can come in if you like—both of you," Sham went on. "I'll see you're all right. We can make a deal." He glanced at me but I looked away. I was waiting for Jane.

"We can make a deal," he urged, unnerved by the silence. "You just do what I tell you. It's my baby." He leaned forward suddenly. "Seventeen million quid," he whispered.

"You don't know nothing," said Jane. She got up. "Here's your baby." She put her into his arms, and then she got out that big bag she'd bought at the drugstore. She took out a bottle of disinfectant and cotton, went over to the dead man, and she began dabbing at his face. The smell of disinfectant filled the little den.

"But he's dead . . ." began Sham. Jane took no notice. She dabbed away until his skin was clean. He had a handsome face. He looked as if he was deep in thought, so deep that even Jane dabbing cold disinfectant on his skin couldn't disturb him. When his face was clean she started on his hands. Then she took the hood of his anorak down and began brushing his hair, his dead hair, with her own brush.

"He was a good man," she said. "He needs looking after, whether he's dead or not."

Sham laughed out loud. He was a gangster, he'd stolen someone's baby. He wasn't a good man!

Jane didn't react. Sham jerked his head at me. "What's up with her?" he demanded.

I shrugged. She was always strange. Jane took no notice. She was straightening up his clothes and making him smart. She glanced back when the baby started making noises again, but she put it out of her mind and got back to her job. Finally she folded his arms over his chest. He looked so peaceful. I stared at him and I thought of all the good things he'd lost.

Jane stood up.

"Come on, Davey." She began to push her way out.

"Wait—wait a minute," said Sham in alarm. You could see him thinking: what had he done wrong? "Where are you going?" he begged.

"Home," said Jane flatly.

Sham looked at me. I knew what he was thinking. My sister might be too good for this but I wouldn't throw away seventeen million pounds. But I was curious. Here was my goody-goody sister who was too stuck-up to steal a stick of licorice, and she was making a play. She had Sham—clever, quick, Sly Sham— not knowing what she was going to do next.

I shrugged. "She's my sister," I said.

Sham was furious. This was all wrong! He'd found the baby, he'd been there when the man had died, he was in charge. There was all that money! He looked so confused, I could have laughed. I glanced at Jane. Maybe I didn't know her as well as I thought.

"You need us," said Jane.

Sham's face went hard.

"If you want me in on this we have to give the baby back," said Jane. "Give it. For free."

As she said this ridiculous thing she took my arm and squeezed it tightly. I stared at her and pulled my arm away but Jane held tightly on, glancing urgently at me to make me wait. Her face was hot and excited as if she might lose her temper or break out in tears any moment.

"Give it? Give it?" squeaked Sham. Give up seventeen million? No one had ever given us anything. Why should we?

"You haven't thought this through," said Jane, trying hard to keep her voice steady. She eased herself down among the crushed boxes and watched him. "Think. How many people are out there looking for this baby? The police. The parents. The gangs. Everyone. It's been on the TV. Everyone knows. Do you think they'll let us get away with it?"

"He told me . . ." began Sham. "We phone, we make an appointment . . ."

"He's not rich, is he, Sham?" said Jane, nodding at the dead man. Sham shrugged. He was prepared to risk anything for that money.

"He told me how. We keep the baby until we get the money, you see," explained Sham urgently. "If they try anything"—he shrugged and made a gesture at his throat—"the baby gets it."

We all turned to look at the baby. She was sitting up in the cardboard box playing with the tape. When she tried to put it

melvin burgess

in her mouth and found she couldn't, she lost her temper. She flung herself back, grunting and jerking.

Jane stared at Sham. He shrugged again, a little, careless gesture. "We don't have to really do it," he said. "We can just say."

"Even if we did get away with it, we'd be hunted down afterward," insisted Jane. "Three kids with all that money . . . How long do you think we'd keep it? If you spend a tenner on fish and chips Mother knows about it and she wants to know where you got it. Look . . ."

She leaned forward and stared into Sham's face. Her eyes were so bright and she was shaking. She wanted it her way so badly she was shaking with it. I didn't join in, I just watched. I'd never seen her like this before.

"Do you know what making good means?" she asked. We looked at each other. Everybody knows what making good means.

"Making good," said Jane. She had to stop and swallow before she went on, she was so choked up. "Listen: there'll be a reward."

Sham had been staring at her as if she had three heads but now he began to understand. He began to shake his head.

"A legal reward. See? We're going to make good. We're going to do it right. We're going to bring the parents back their poor little lost baby. We're the good guys. We're going to look after that baby—it's going to be our little baby, our little sister, while we have it. And we're going to do it together and we're going to trust one another, like the man said. We're the good guys."

She held out her hand and touched the baby on the cheek. Sham stared at her hand and shook his head.

"Making good," she said. "Not being greedy. Not being dirty. Doing someone a good turn and being rewarded for it."

Sham looked at me out of the corner of his eye to see what I thought about it.

"That's what the man said," I said haltingly.

"But that was just a trick," cried Sham. "You know that don't you, Fly?" He was desperate. He needed us and he knew it but Jane was throwing it all away. "How much do you think they'll give to rubbish kids?" He stared at her, willing her to understand. "No one gives anything unless they have to," he explained.

Jane shook her head. "We don't have to be like that. It's a chance, see? We can make it out of here the right way—so we stay out. We don't have to take the Tip with us. Do you see?" she pleaded with me.

"Sure," I said. I was embarrassed.

"It won't be enough," urged Sham. "Seventeen million is enough for everyone, but a reward . . . They don't have to give us anything."

"We'll just have to trust them."

Sham stared. "Seventeen million pounds," he said, as if it was a spell. He really couldn't believe she was going to throw it away. He sat there shaking his head. "No," he said. "No, no, no . . ."

But she had strength, my sister. She wanted that chance so badly, more than anyone she wanted that chance. I really believe that if all that seventeen million was there by our sides Jane would have chucked it into the wind—just to keep herself clean.

Sham was in agony. "Fly Pie," he groaned. "Make her see sense—she's your sister. . . ."

I wanted to be on her side. Maybe a few years back, when I was small . . . I mean, I was impressed by the way she was handling it. I was impressed by what she said. But there was Sham watching us and I knew that the world wasn't like that.

All that talk about people giving things away—that was just pie in the sky. I was thinking about the money. There was a wallet, and the wallet was full of dreams. . . .

I couldn't look at her. I was just doing a job, my voice said. I was earning money—a thousand pounds to get my sister to that man to doctor him up. All I wanted to do was take my money around to Luke and get him to buy me out. I'd already made good, I said. What Sham and Jane did was their business. I wanted my money, now. And then I wanted to get out.

Sham kept interrupting—that the man was dead and everything had changed.

Jane said, "Give me the money, Sham."

"He's not getting that," exclaimed Sham.

Jane held out her hand. "Trust me," she said.

Sham snorted. He was almost laughing. Who did she think she was? He had the money, he had nothing to gain. And yet—it was a funny thing—he did trust her. We all trusted Jane. She was all wrong, she thought you could make good just by keeping your nose clean. But she didn't lie and she didn't steal and if she said you could trust her you knew you could.

Sham dug in his pocket and took out the wallet. He weighed it in his hand, then handed it over to her. I was amazed. I think he was, too. Maybe he was curious to see what she was going to do.

Jane took the money out of its leather wrap and started counting—one hundred, two hundred, three hundred . . . By the time she got to one thousand there was barely any left. I picked it up and looked in the little flaps in the sides and everywhere, but there couldn't have been more than a hundred left. It wasn't that Sham had helped himself. The pile in front of me was as big as it had ever been. I'd thought there were thousands and thousands of pounds there.

"But I thought . . ."

"Take your money, Fly Pie," said my sister. I looked at her. She never called me Fly Pie. Then I shrugged. I started stuffing the money in my trousers.

"Hey, what you doing?" demanded Sham starting forward. But Jane held his arm.

"You know," she mused, "it'll be pretty difficult for Sham and me to find the baby's parents now you've got all the money. But a deal's a deal. Take it and go, Fly Pie."

I didn't go. I stared sulkily at her.

"One thing," she said. She pushed her hair out of her eyes. "Look at me, Fly Pie. Am I a pretty girl? Would you say I'm pretty?"

I didn't want to look. I didn't need to. My sister's pretty enough.

She flicked at the hem of her little dress with her fingers. "What's a girl like me doing on the street at that time of night dressed up like this?" she asked me. She was looking steadily at me. Now I managed to look back at her. She had lipstick on. I'd not noticed that before. And makeup. And those pretty clothes. My sister never wore clothes like that. She hated that sort of thing. Anyway, it wasn't allowed—Mother never let her girls wear makeup and they certainly never had clothes like that.

I knew suddenly then. She'd been sold on.

"She's a prossie," said Sham.

Jane flinched. She watched me.

"But Mother said you wouldn't . . ."

Jane shook her head. "Mother says," she jeered. She stared at me until I dropped my eyes—as if it was me who'd done those shameful things.

"Mother says Jane Shelly'll get a good job," she said. "Mother says Fly Pie is going to be a baker's boy. Mother says . . ."

She was a good girl. She'd kept herself decent, not like the other girls, who did things with whoever wanted them. She was proud. She worked harder than anyone. You could trust her. She'd earned her chance, not like the rest of us.

Those things don't matter. She was the same as everyone and now she was selling herself to old men for a few quid a go because being young and pretty was all she had after all. She'd been hanging around by the speakers at the street fair to make it difficult for them to pick her up. We'd run out of the fair at the back in case her pimp caught her. Jane wasn't going to marry a good man with a job, or get work in a nice clean little shop anymore. She was going to stand out at night and do it in doorways, and get beaten up every night she didn't bring back enough money. Someone had paid money for her and now he owned her, and everything she had was his.

"Okay," I said. I took the money out and gave it to her. I only did it because I felt sorry for her.

Jane gave me an odd glance—grateful and hateful at the same time. I couldn't meet her eye. It wasn't her fault, but I'd been proud of her before that. Still, she'd done what she wanted. She'd turned everything right around in a circle and she was still herself. She scooped up the money and held it out to Sham. "You're our treasurer," she told him shakily. "You look after the money for all of us." She did that to show him that she'd be fair all the way, right down to giving Sham Shelly money, which no one in their right mind would do.

"Okay," said Sham. He reached out but she pulled it back.

"We do it my way. Okay?"

Sham pursed his lips. He'd made a mistake giving her the money after all. "If there's a reward," he said. "If not . . ." He shrugged.

"There will be," said Jane. "Deal?"

"Deal," said Sham.

She held out the money again. He leaned forward, his hand gliding down and putting the money in his pocket. "I'll be treasurer, I'll look after it—for us all."

five

Now we made plans—real plans. Jane did, anyway. We had to get away from the Tip. We planned to hide in Santy, the squatter city on the other side of the dump. There were always new people turning up there, people coming to a better life— so they thought. Once we'd found a place to stay we could start thinking about getting the reward. It wasn't going to be easy. We couldn't go to the police—they'd just take the baby and claim the reward themselves. We had to find out who the parents were, and how to get in touch with them and work out some sort of way of getting the baby to them.

We had all that to come. Right now we had to wait. They'd be looking for us already . . . Mother Shelly's Big Boys. We belonged to Mother Shelly and she didn't like her property to go missing. The man who'd bought Jane would have been in touch with her by now and she wouldn't like that either. It didn't do her prices any good to have girls she sold running off. She'd have Shiner and Duck and the others scouring the Tip and the shops and the cinemas and TV stands and amusement arcades, and she'd keep at it half the night if she had to. We'd have to wait until three or four in the morning to be safe.

It was bad in there with the dead man. You couldn't stop feeling that he was suddenly going to sit up and say something. It was his baby, after all. In the end Jane wrapped him up in boxes like a sort of coffin and she said a little prayer over him. The next day or so when the bulldozers came, they'd find him. Someone would put two and two together.

Jane talked and talked. She went on and on. She wanted us to see it her way. As she talked, she got more and more certain about it.

She said we had to behave like proper people. People didn't judge you by what you did, she said—they judged you by what you were inside. We just had to be *like* that enough and the good would come without us even trying.

I'd heard it all before. What good had it done her? But she kept on and on and I listened until it really began to seem that hers was the right way and that all the hard things I'd learned and seen were nothing.

But then I'd see Sham sitting there. He didn't argue. He just sat and watched with his big eyes and never said a word. He needed us because he couldn't look after the baby on his own all the time, but that didn't change anything. He'd gone along with it because he had to. I knew Sham. He was waiting for his chance. Jane was going to trust him as much as she trusted me but I knew that all he wanted to be was a big crook, the bigger the better, and get money and respect out of people whether they wanted to give it or not.

At last Jane lay down and closed her eyes. I could smell perfume on her. It was too dark to see by then but I remembered that skimpy little dress with her legs and shoulders bare and her face made up, and it didn't seem like my sister lying there. She lay down like some big strange animal trying to get to sleep. I thought of what had happened to her and I was humiliated. We all knew she wasn't fit for that sort of thing. Mother Shelly knew it. She'd been sold as a prossie and now she was another person.

I went up and tickled her hand. She squeezed it back.

"We're on our way, Davey," she said.

"We're going to get out, " I whispered. I was embarrassed to cuddle her with Sham sitting just a few feet away but I lay down next to her. I tried to ignore him and wriggled close, as if I could turn her back into a kid the way it used to be. But nothing was going to be the same again.

So far we'd been lucky but things were moving. The weather was changing. It was spitting gusts when dark fell, but later on the wind blew up. You could hear the cardboard boxes banging about the yard and rolling around on top of us. The noise got louder and louder. It was frightening. You wouldn't believe the noises the wind could make when it had all those boxes to play with. It was crashing and booming and banging and whistling and shrieking. We crouched down like mice. The whole heap was shaking, the noise was tremendous. And suddenly the boxes blew away above us. Everything went flying off into the darkness and we were hanging on to the ground, trying to get out of the way.

I could see the dead man coming out of his cardboard as if he were alive. Sham snatched the baby and we all went haring along, diving and ducking the flying boxes, toward the old garages at the edge of the yard.

We tried to stay there but the boxes kept blowing in so we made another run and got to a derelict little building that still had doors. We slammed the door behind us but the boxes were still making the most enormous noise. The baby hated it; she was jerking and trying to scream but of course she couldn't because of the tape on her mouth. Jane took it off and tried to feed her, but the baby just gargled on the milk and howled, so we made her put some more tape on.

"The Big Boys won't be out in this," Jane insisted.

"Don't you believe it," said Sham. He was right. Mother looked after her Big Boys but they had to do everything she said.

We tried to settle down but it was impossible. Sham kept crawling out to see his watch by the flashes of moonlight and the time crawled by. Things got a bit better when the baby took another bottle and went to sleep. The wind was still big, but not so big. We began to relax again.

We should have known better. Trouble comes whether you expect it or not. With all the noise there could have been anything outside. As it was, it was Shiner.

He knew we were there, he must have been looking in through the window. He just kicked the door open and there he was.

"I knew you'd be round here somewhere," he said grimly. "You're for it, you little bastards." Then he saw the baby and stopped in his tracks.

"Man! What's that?" he yelped.

I have to hand it to Sham. I'd never have dared but he didn't waste a second. He's only a little squirt but he dived straight in and got around Shiner's legs. The big boy waved his arms and toppled and hit the ground with a crack. He was up quick enough though. He was twice as big as any of us and he kicked Sham off him halfway across the room. Then Jane was there clawing at his face and before I knew it, I was on his back, pulling his hair and grabbing his neck.

It was terrifying. Shiner was sixteen, big and vicious. You couldn't hurt him, all you could do was wrap yourself around him and hope someone else was doing the business. Jane was hugging his neck from the front, I was hugging his neck from the back. We were both up off the ground and he was staggering to and fro pulling at our arms saying, "Get off, get off, will yer?" He sounded surprised.

Then Sham got hold of a piece of wood and started cracking at his shins with it. Shiner couldn't see a thing because of Jane round his neck, and he began stepping and dancing about like a bear trying to kick its boots off. He kept gargling where we squeezed his neck and yelling "Watch it, watch it!" whenever he could snatch a breath.

Then he lost his temper and fell over. Sham started whacking him with the stick and missing and getting me and Jane instead because he was thrashing about so much. There was a really nasty moment when Shiner got mad. He got back on his feet and he was swinging at us and we were flying and bouncing off the walls. But we got dirty. There were feet and sticks and stones everywhere and Shiner hit the ground. That was the end of it. Sham got wrapped around his feet, I had his arm halfway up his back and Jane was banging away on his head with a bit of wood as hard as she could.

"Okay, okay, stop it, stop it!" Shiner screamed.

Jane carried on. He couldn't move a muscle but she didn't seem to notice. She just went on, bang, bang, bang! as hard as she could.

There was a pause while we stared at her.

"Jane!" Sham yelled. She stared at him

"Get those sacks and tear 'em up," he ordered. There was a heap of sacks in the corner we'd been trying to sleep on. Shiner didn't dare move a muscle after what she'd done but we had a hell of a job tearing them up. Still, we managed to wrap his feet up and wrap a few more around his body and arms. Then we found some nylon rope and the three of us tied him up and wrapped the rope around and around until he looked like some sort of party game.

We stood around panting. We were amazed at what we'd done. When Sham snorted I jumped, I was so nervous. He was laughing! I glared at him but then I saw what he meant. Here was the great Shiner wrapped up from head to foot so he couldn't move a finger and glaring at us over the top of his rope. There was a big knot on top of his head and he looked like nothing more than a great, big rabbit. Pretty soon we were wetting ourselves. I could see his eyes bright in the pale light from the little lamps in the yard. There was wet glistening in his hair where Jane had hit him with the stick.

Then I was frightened again. "What'll we do, what'll we do?" I begged.

Sham said, "Kill him."

There was a horrible silence.

"You're mad," said Shiner in a surprised voice.

Jane looked at Sham, a curious little look. "Would you do that?" she asked him.

Sham said, "You leave me alone with him for ten minutes and see."

I knew what he meant. Shiner was a brute. I'd never thought about it because it seemed the only way he could be, but now that he was trussed up and helpless on the floor in front of me I could have done anything to him.

"This is a bad start," said Jane. "We have to make the best of it. We stick to our plan. We wait till it's late then we head off into town. Right?"

That wasn't the plan, of course. She said that for Shiner's benefit.

"I say kill him," said Sham. "He'll tell, won't he?"

He and Jane began to argue over it. Jane's wasn't a good plan because the workmen would find him the next morning and let him loose. They might call the police; Shiner might tell the gangs. At the least he'd tell Mother and the news would be out that Jane, Fly Pie and Sly Sham had the seventeen-million-pound baby. But killing someone . . . It went on all the time, we knew that. But we were kids. None of us had done it. Sham argued it out, but in the end even he wasn't ready for that; not yet.

The waiting was worse now. We had hours to go. After a bit, Shiner began to talk but we couldn't listen to what he had to say so we gagged him with the sacks.

It was very late when we finally felt safe to set off. The baby had fallen asleep with the bottle in her mouth. Jane smoothed another strip of tape over her mouth to be on the safe side, and she woke up and struggled but it was too late to take it off then. We checked that Shiner was tied up tight and gagged. I don't think we were too careful making sure he wasn't tied too tight. Then we stepped out into the wind.

That business with Shiner was bad luck but it gave us a boost. He was the most famous of the Big Boys. If we could beat him, we could do anything. We were on our way!

There was a bit of a moon and some way off we could see the street lamps and little lights in the yards of the Tip office buildings. We left the boxes rumbling around the yard and got out onto the Tip proper. It was weird. I'd never seen the Tip like that before. It was always busy—kids working for the Mothers, all the others who live on it and off it, the workmen, the tourists who come to see the people who live off rubbish. But when we crept out that night there was nothing. Just cold and darkness and the wind flinging rubbish along the ground. After ten minutes we heard a noise behind us—bang, bang, bang, it went.

"Shiner," said Sham in a disgusted voice. He'd somehow got over to the door and he was banging at it with his feet to get attention.

It was hard going in the dark. Jane was crippled in her high heels, so she knocked them off with a piece of metal. But she was still hobbling along because the shoes were bent. She looked so funny, like a duck. We laughed, but I didn't realize till later what it must have been like for her. She had to tie some cardboard around her to keep warm because she was wearing almost nothing. Then we made our way onto the dirt road that led up from the dump toward the landfill where they bury the old rubbish. Up there, where everything was bulldozed flat, the going was a lot easier.

The road took us higher and higher. Soon we could look over our shoulders and see the city spread out behind us— orange and white and pearly pink lights that blurred into a smoggy haze in the distance. They looked pretty like that. Above us was a little moon and a few stars, sliding in and out behind the clouds. The wind was big up there and it carried the smells of London to us—smoke and traffic fumes, the Tip—all the smells of fifteen million people living in a rabbit hutch.

Right on the top, where the old valley is filled in, it's a flat desert of rutted clay with bits of iron or wire or plastic sticking out of the ground. They reckon one day they're going to cover it with earth and make a garden. They can do anything if they want to. Soon we could see the other city—the squatters' city. It lay spread out below us, a thin spangle of lights. It was still a long way off.

Jane was hobbling along in those shoes, with the cold wind flicking that little dress. She clutched the baby to her breast and she was muttering away to herself as if she was in a dream. Sometimes she bent down to croon something to the baby, but I don't know who the rest of it was for. I wondered how long since she'd been sold on—how many nights, how many customers?

Jane stopped. The wind was hard, whistling past our ears and past the bits of iron and things sticking out of the clay. The baby was grunting in her arms.

"She's had that tape on long enough," Jane said. "She's going to be our baby sister like I said." No one said anything. Jane reached down and ripped the tape off.

The baby stared at her. You could see even in that light how pale she was where the tape had been. She just stared up at Jane, suddenly wide awake, hurt. Then a big black hole opened in the middle of her face. And she screamed—and she screamed and screamed and screamed. It was so loud it seemed to split the air.

"Give her her bottle," demanded Sham, looking all around as if he expected the dead to jump out of the ground.

"Let her cry it out," said Jane calmly.

"No, no, they'll hear!" I cried. It was such a noise, you felt you'd do anything to stop that noise. But Jane just put the baby on her shoulder and patted her back.

"That's better," she said. "There, that's better." I was sure every living soul in the two cities must have heard it. She was choking and sobbing and wailing and beating and thrashing about—all the tears that had been stuck behind the tape came tumbling out. Every now and then she'd run out of air and bend herself right back screaming silently, and you thought she'd break her back. Then she'd suck up an enormous breath and it'd start all over again.

the baby and fly pie

"Someone'll hear!" cried Sham. When the baby heard his voice, she turned and put out her arms to him. She wanted Sham. Jane handed her over and the baby buried her head on Sham's shoulder and sobbed harder than ever.

Sham started to walk up and down. "There, there—there, there . . ." he murmured, while the baby held onto his neck and screamed. Jane watched him. She was jealous, I think.

"You're her little father," she said to Sham. "You were the first one to care for her after what they did."

Sham looked frightened but he kept on patting her and walking up and down, up and down. It went on for ages. Then at last the baby began to hiccup and cough. Slowly she began to settle down and then she fell asleep, suddenly, on Sham's shoulder.

"There," said Jane. She was proud of him! Sham looked at her and down to the baby, but you could never guess what he was thinking. The baby slept most of the time after that, even though she was jogged about in our arms. But every now and then she woke up and screamed suddenly as if she was lost, and then we scurried on fast.

Halfway down the hill from the landfill was a tall fence. On the other side the squatter city began. We call it Santy, but the people who live there have another name for it. Most of the toilets are just holes in the ground and they hardly ever get cleaned out. Some people can't even be bothered to go there, and do it behind their shacks or even in the streets if it's dark. That's how it gets its nickname—Shitty City.

People come from all over the world to live in London but this is as far as most of them get. It's bigger than most proper cities, except London, of course. The new people live far out, away from the fence. They build tents or shacks or benders, or live in vans and cars. They settle down and wait for the good times to come. They go tramping off into London to look for them. And sometimes, the good times do come. But for most of them there's nothing to do and not enough to eat and they're cold and wet in the winter. And yet they always stay, even though they might have been better off where they came from. For some reason, it's better to be poor on the edge of London than better off anywhere else.

Here by the fence it had been settled for a long time and people had things sorted—decent houses and latrines and so on. The shacks went right up to the fence—some of them even used the fence as a wall of their house. On the other side was nothing. People are always trying to set up on the other side of the fence but every morning they get beaten off by guards with dogs and guns. One day, the government wants to build proper houses or offices there, and once the squatters get settled it's hard to move them on.

We climbed over the fence, handing the baby up from one to the other, and began picking our way through the crowded muddle of shacks, sheds and tents. It smelled of smoke and damp rubbish. It was dark—just one or two little lamps hung by people's doors. They'd put grit and gravel on the tracks to keep the wet down but it was trodden to mud anyway. Some of the places were shops with big shutters up on the windows and outside one I found balls of screwed-up newspaper and I could smell what that place sold—fish and chips! I remembered—I was starving! I picked up some of the paper and poked about inside for scraps. Jane was cross.

"Put it down, dirty," she snapped, slapping the paper out of my hand. I stared at her. It wasn't dirty, it was all wrapped up. It tasted good.

"We don't need other people's scraps, not now," she insisted.

the baby and fly pie

"I'm hungry," I said.

Sham said, "We eat what we can." He bent down and began to go through the paper bundles himself, looking at her out of the corner of his eye to see what she did. He wanted to show her she wasn't the boss, not as far as he was concerned. I picked mine back up and began licking up the little scraps of batter and chips.

Jane watched for a second, then she shrugged. "All right— just for now." She was hungry too and she joined in with us— all three of us rustling through the paper balls outside the dark shop, like a bunch of dogs. The baby was asleep, wrapped in the sack the gunman had her in, but she cried briefly as Jane bent down. Then we heard someone moving inside the shop and we ran off.

We ran into a man hurrying along the muddy track. He stopped to stare at us—especially at Jane. She'd thrown away her cardboard wrapping when we got into Santy. It was a cold night and there she was wearing a tiny party dress and holding a baby.

"What're you doing here?" he demanded.

"We lost our mum," said Jane, looking him straight in the face. "We're new here," she added.

The man pointed away. "You belong over there in the camps," he said. That's what the people who were established called the edges of the squatter city. "This land's taken, there's no more room. If you're new, you go that way. Do you get me?" He pointed away and said again, angrily, "This land is taken."

"We're only looking," complained Jane.

"No one wants new people, not around here," said the man again. He stared at us and then walked off, disappearing into the black night quickly. Jane made a face after him.

"No one wants new people around here," she mimicked and we sniggered. But the man must have heard.

"You'd better get out quick. There's a Squad out tonight, looking for kids like you," he snapped.

That shut us up. We heard him walking away through the mud and gravel. We peered about. So many dark corners . . .

"I thought they never had Squads in Santy," said Sham.

"He's just scaring us," said Jane. "Wants to get us out."

"They have Squads everywhere," I whined.

"Don't be daft. Who'd pay 'em?" demanded Jane briskly. She pushed us forward, deeper into the squatter city.

We went on our way more quietly than ever. I could have strangled that baby. She kept waking up and squealing. Sham disappeared quick around some corner when she woke up and I followed him, even though Jane looked at me in disgust. She wouldn't put that tape back, even though we begged her to— even though she must have been as scared as the rest of us.

We walked for ages. You couldn't see where you were. People had built their homes higgledy-piggledy, one next to the other, and the streets curled and ran to and fro—you couldn't keep in the same direction if you wanted to. Sometimes we came out on top of a hill and we could see by the moonlight which way was in and which way was out, but most of the time we were just lost.

We were still wandering around when it got light. In the end we found a little row of shops and sat down on the steps to wait for them to open. Me and Sham did, anyway, Jane got up after a couple of minutes and began to hobble up and down in her bent duck's shoes.

"What's the matter?" I asked her.

"I'm bloody freezing, that's what's the matter," she hissed.

the baby and fly pie

"You didn't say," I said. Then I saw how she was limping as she trotted up and down. Those broken shoes had blistered her feet but she hadn't said a word. "Couldn't you find a blanket or something on the way?" I asked her. You could always pick something up like that on the streets or the Tip.

"There wasn't any," she said. "There's nothing around here."

I thought it had been too dark, or that she hadn't looked hard enough. There's always something. We took it in turns with my coat.

Sham had put the baby down next to him. He curled up around her in his big brown coat and went to sleep.

Jane stopped hopping about to look at him. "Look at him, isn't it sweet? Who'd have thought he knew about babies. . . ."

After a bit I got scared and I said to Jane, "Shouldn't we be hiding?"

She wrapped her arms about herself and shook her head. "No one's going to think three kids have a baby like that. We just have to face it out, Davey."

I sat a while watching Sham and the baby while Jane trotted up and down. Then I think I must have gone to sleep too because the next thing I knew the shop was open and Jane was talking on the steps to a woman.

I thought—the day's begun. They'd be finding Shiner about now.

"We only want to buy something—we've been waiting," Jane was saying. "We've been out all night. . . ."

The shopkeeper was looking at Jane in her skimpy little dress and those ridiculous broken shoes. She didn't seem to like the idea of us buying things in her shop. She turned away and began opening the shutters.

melvin burgess
66

"We need some clothes—a coat and things," said Jane. "We've got money, haven't we?" she appealed to us.

"Oh, yeah, we can pay," I said. Sham still lay on the wooden steps cradling the baby. He looked sulky.

"We don't need to spend money on clothes," he said.

"Sham, I'm freezing cold, I can't go around like this," Jane begged.

"We can find throw outs," said Sham.

The woman snorted. "No one throws anything away here," she said sourly.

"Sham," pleaded Jane. She crouched down to him. "We're going to have to spend a lot more before we're through," she hissed. He was embarrassing her. Sham looked away. The baby began to sniffle and the woman looked at her. Sham hid her away in the folds of his coat.

"We ought to go," he said. But Jane wasn't budging and finally he fished around in his coat and brought out ten pounds.

I was watching. I saw something else tucked away in there.

"You'll need more than that," said the woman scornfully. She went back into the shop. Jane stood up painfully. "We'll need food, too. We're not on the Tip now, Sham. Out here you have to buy things," She hobbled after the woman into the shop.

I leaned forward. "What happened to the gun, Sham?" I asked, glancing down at his coat. I'd seen something heavy and awkward under there. That man had a gun. Where was it now?

He looked coolly at me. "We'll need it," he said. "Someone's got to protect us." He nodded at the shop after Jane. "She won't."

I didn't say any more about it just then. I was about to follow Jane into the shop but Sham held my arm.

"She's wrong," he said. "She's wrong, and you know it."

I pulled away. I didn't want to think about it.

"She's wrong," insisted Sham. "Listen. We can do it together. Fifty-fifty. Together . . ."

"She's my sister," I said. I began to move off.

"I'm not asking you to dump her," urged Sham. "You can come back for her when we've got the money. Seventeen million. You think. Think about *that*. You can get her anything you want. You can rescue her. I can do it but I need your help. She hasn't got what it takes. . . ."

I could hear Jane talking to the shop woman. Sham was right, of course. This wasn't Jane's thing but it was just what Sham was good at. He knew how people were, how to make them do what he wanted, how to get what he wanted. I was surprised by the way my sister had handled Sham, but that didn't change the facts.

"She didn't even make it to be a housewife," said Sham.

But—she was my sister. Where did it leave her if I walked off right now with Sham and the baby and left her in her broken shoes and her prossie clothes? You didn't do that to your own sister.

I wasn't ready to dump her. Not yet. And I wasn't ready to trust Sly Sham, either.

"I'll think about it," I said.

"Don't think about it too long," advised Sham. He let go of my arm and sat down on the steps as I followed Jane inside.

We had a terrible job getting the money out of him. The woman wanted seventy pounds for a pair of patched trousers, an old coat and a pair of second-hand boots! They were awful old things, too—we could pick up better stuff than that any day on the Tips. Jane threw in her posh little dress as well and got the price down to fifty. Sham didn't like it but even he could see we couldn't let her wander around looking like she did. He didn't care about her being cold, but she was attracting attention. She looked like—what she was.

We bought bread and biscuits, some more milk which the woman warmed up for us and a few other things, like pacifiers for the baby. They really worked later on and I wished we'd had them before. Jane told the woman we'd been booted out of our house in London and that we'd got separated from our parents on the journey over to Santy.

The woman told us, "You can buy things in the camps to make a shelter until you find your people. But there's no room here. . . ." She shook her head firmly. "Not an inch. You'd better go quick," she added. "People don't like new faces with nowhere to go hanging around. There's no space at all, you see," she repeated.

"Do you get Squads here?" I asked her.

"Oh, yes, we get Squads," she said, watching me. "We pay 'em to keep the place clean. But not in the camps. You go there. You'll be safe there."

"Do you believe her?" I asked Jane when we got outside.

She made a face and shook her head. But we were glad to get away.

The bus left from what that woman called the High Street, although it was just a dirt road. Jane began to feed the baby as we waited but Sham insisted on doing it. She gave in easily enough. The way she thought was, if you wanted to hold a baby you couldn't be all bad.

"You're so good with her, Sham, you're so good," she kept saying. Sham glanced up and smiled shyly. But I was cross. He wasn't interested in feeding her. He just wanted to make sure she took to him in case he had to look after her on his own.

After half an hour an old van with some seats in the back

turned up. We climbed on and paid our fares and away it drove over the bumpy, potholed road, past the wooden shacks and out to the edges of the camp. As we went further out the houses got poorer and poorer. Soon all those solid-looking shacks were gone and we were driving past tents and sheds and all sorts of crazy-looking shelters. It was over an hour before the driver beckoned to us.

We climbed out into the mud and he drove off.

In front of us was a field, and in it sprouted lean-tos and tents and polythene humps and shacks made of mud and sticks and tin and straw—you name it. I even saw places made out of cardboard.

The baby had slept all the way on the bus but now she woke up and began yelling. I hated that noise, it made everyone look. Sham had had enough of her too, and he gave her to Jane, who tucked her down the front of her big coat so she could look out over the top. She liked that. She looked so funny with her bald little head peeping out, grinning all lopsided when she saw us watching, she made us laugh. And we felt good because we'd made the baby happy again.

Then we began looking for a place to build our new home.

We found an empty space in a hollow. Of course Sham didn't want to spend money on stuff to build our camp. He still thought we could find something, so we had to go off and look, but that shop woman was right. No one threw away anything here. There wasn't a stick or a scrap. I found some piles of rubbish but the rubbish here really was rubbish. . . . I poked about but it was all useless. Sham tried to pull a piece of polythene off one of the buildings that looked as though it might be empty, but a man came out and chased him until he caught him and gave him a real hard clout around the head. He knocked Sham right off his feet.

"What do you mean, pinching people's homes?" he yelled. He was really cross. Sham was trying hard not to cry. He hated to cry. That convinced him that we had to buy what we needed.

We were only going to be there a while, so we just bought sticks and polythene and a pile of old blankets. The shop man charged us forty-five pounds! I could have cried because that sort of thing is everywhere on the Tip, and if we'd known we could have brought a mountain of it with us. But we didn't know, so we had to spend the money. We stuck the sticks in the ground and draped the polythene over them. We dug up some earth to weigh the polythene down, put some more polythene on the floor and laid the blankets on top of that. And that was our house.

six

We got ready just in time. The wind blew cold and it got dark. The rain began slowly but it quickly got hard and we all dashed under cover. We wrapped ourselves in blankets and watched as everyone ran.

It really pelted down for a few minutes. We peeked through the polythene as the shop man ran out to pull down a big awning over the chairs and things he had outside the shop. He had a pole with a hook on it. The awning came down with a big thump and the whole front of the shop swayed and bounced as if it was going to fall down. The man cringed away for a second before he ran back inside.

The water began to flow in underneath our little tent and in a minute we were all trying to pile the blankets and the baby in a dry corner. The baby thought it was great fun. She kept trying to splash in the puddles.

"You've come down in the world, you have," Jane said, lifting her up in the air. The baby gave her that wobbly smile and tried to grab her nose. Jane let her suck her nose and we all laughed.

"That baby sucks everything," laughed Sham.

Jane's nose was all wet and so was her hair where the rain had got her. "We've got our own place," she said proudly.

Sham looked crookedly at her, his smile fading. He said, "Piece of plastic on a stick."

"We got out, didn't we?" Jane said. She tucked her hair behind her ear and stared at him. "No one's going to tell you what to do now—when to go to bed, when to eat, nothing. You don't have to go and get counted. This is ours. It's a start."

"It's less than we had," complained Sham. "We're further away from town, where the action is." He wasn't being fair. He was watching Jane in that close way of his.

Jane glanced at me but I looked away. She leaned forward as if she could press her words into him. "What do you have to look at it like that for? It's going right. We got away. We have a base. We've got money to keep us going. Next thing is to find out where to telephone. Who the baby is, who her parents are. We couldn't stay on the Tip, you know that. If we'd gone into town we'd have had to rent somewhere and what do you think that would have cost?"

Sham looked out across the wet fields, across the glistening sheets of polythene and corrugated iron. He didn't answer.

"It's all wrong," he said.

It *was* all wrong—trusting people to do you a favor if you did one for them. It was asking for trouble but I hated him for saying so.

"Don't say that," I told him. "You'll bring us bad luck."

Jane glanced at me but I wouldn't meet her eye. I didn't know where I stood. I only knew that Sham would never believe what she wanted. Sham had only ever wanted to make it by being better, sharper, harder, quicker. And here she was telling him to be nice!

the baby and fly pie

"Okay," said Jane. "We'll ring them up and see what they say, okay? See if they'll offer us something. A reward. That way we'll find out. Okay?"

Sham pulled his blanket from a puddle that was forming underneath him. He made a face. "They can say whatever they like, can't they?" he said. He kept glancing at me. He was speaking to Jane but it was me he was telling. I was cross at him for putting me on the spot.

That's when I remembered what I'd seen in his pocket that morning. I said at once, "He's got the gun, too."

"What gun?" She tensed up. "We don't need guns," she said.

Sham stared blandly at me. He patted his pocket. "We may need it. I picked it up—to protect us," he said.

Jane stared at his pocket.

"He's got everything," I said. "The money, the gun. Everything."

"That's right," said Jane. "You've seen me play fair. Now you play fair. You have the money or the gun—one or the other."

Sham shook his head.

"I gave you the money back," she insisted. "You play fair with us." She looked at him as if she could burn him up.

"Are you going to walk out?" he jeered.

Jane shook her head. "That was before. We made a deal. You have to stick to our deals, can't you see that?"

There was a long pause. Sham ended it by taking out the wallet and putting it on the ground.

"If you've got the gun, you've got the money, too, in the end," he said. He looked at her coolly. Jane picked it up and tucked it in her trousers.

"I won't let you down, Sham, even though you said that—

even if you do it." She stared at him. Sham looked down and hid his face. I'd never seen him hide his face before. It was as if she'd taken everything away from him, because she was more prepared to let him shoot her than he was to do it.

When the rain let up we went out to explore. We needed to see how things worked and find out about the kidnapping. Jane stayed behind to watch the tent and baby-sit.

"Did you really have a baby of your own?" I asked Sham as we walked across the puddles and trodden mud.

Sham turned to look carefully at me with his deep brown eyes, as if he could find out everything he needed to know just by looking. I was only curious.

"My mum used to go out and leave me to look after him," he said.

"When was that, then?" Sham had been with Mother Shelly as long as I could remember.

"When I was little."

Then I wanted to know. "What happened to him?"

"He got lost."

"How?" He turned again to look carefully at me. Now I felt as if I was stealing from him. But he didn't say anything.

"What was it like—having a mum and dad and all that?" I asked jealously.

"I don't know," said Sham. And he wouldn't say any more.

At first sight the whole camp looked like a sort of filthy Tip with the rubbish spread out all over instead of heaped up. But people lived in this rubbish. The cloudburst had turned the place into a mudbath. People were out sweeping muddy streams away from their homes and wiping their tents clean where the dirt had splashed up. We split up. Sham went off in the direction of the shop to see what he could steal. I wandered off around the houses. Neither of us could really believe there was nothing to find lying around somewhere.

I spent ages at it but there really was nothing, not a stick or a scrap of paper that didn't belong to someone. I gave it up and started hanging around trying to overhear something about the kidnapping. No one was talking about it, though. All the radios were playing music. I found a little house with an aerial on it and I could hear the TV on inside. I kept coming back and in the end I was lucky—the news was on. I leaned against the outside wall and kept my ears open. But someone came out and chased me off so that was no use either.

I was on my way home when I saw the old man. He was a big fat old man in his trousers and shirt, sitting in an armchair on a wooden platform half in, half outside. His home was a clever-looking thing, a sort of hangar of branches and polythene and carpet, plastered in mud and then covered again with polythene. It was made of layers like that, and inside there were strings with pots and pans and bits of machinery and other stuff hanging in the air. The floor was raised high up. He had an enormous beard that went right around his face and he would have looked like Santa Claus except that there was an enormous yellow stain in the middle of it from cigarettes. He was sitting there up in the air on his platform floor like the King of Somewhere and Something and he was reading a newspaper.

I wanted that newspaper. Jane could read it. She could find out.

I hung about to one side out of sight. The old man was puffing and blowing, although he wasn't doing much. He didn't have any teeth and he kept squashing his face up. He had a pair of reading glasses on his nose and those and the slippers on his feet made him look as if he was living in a proper house and not in a heap of rubbish at all.

After a long time he leaned back, sighed, and put the newspaper down by the side of his chair. He leaned briefly down by the other side to pick up a can of beer—and I was there. I grabbed the newspaper and went skidding off through the mud. He heard me, of course, and let out a shout, but I was already gone. I glanced back and saw him lumbering down from his platform. But he was still in his slippers—imagine wearing slippers in a place like that!—and he'd only taken a few steps before he realized he was standing in a puddle. He glanced down and bellowed.

"Bloody kids!" he roared. Then he took the slippers off, flung them into his shack and took off after me barefoot.

I lost him quickly; he was big and slow, splashing like a bear in the mud and puddles. I went the wrong way to lead him astray, and then I doubled back and made my way to our place. Not before I flicked through the paper, though. There was a picture of our baby on the second page.

Jane had put down a sheet of polythene outside the tent and the baby was sitting on it. She had a jam jar and she was busy putting sticks and bits of dirt into it. Jane sat on a stone nearby, gazing out across the muddy shacks and tents. She looked vacant, faraway. She frowned at the newspaper when I gave it to her.

"You can read it, can't you?" I said.

Jane didn't reply. She smoothed it down in front of her. She'd taught herself to read. She stayed in and pored over books and learned how while the rest of us were out wasting time. But she didn't seem so sure of herself now. She'd found the picture of the baby and she grinned, then peered anxiously about to make sure no one was watching. She ran her finger along the lines of words.

the baby and fly pie

"What's it say?" I begged.

"Just a minute—the words are so little . . ." she muttered and screwed up her face. "The words are so long," she said. There was a long pause and then she rubbed her face and sat up.

"You said you could read," I said angrily.

"It's bloody hard, it's a posh paper." She glared at the paper for showing her up like that.

"You said you could read," I said again. I kicked at the stupid paper. It had everything we wanted to know! I felt like ripping it to bits. When she heard the paper crackle, the baby smiled her silly loopy smile and reached out to hit at it with her stick.

"Can't you even read her name?" I asked Jane. What was the point of her staying in all that time? It was stupid calling the baby "the baby" all the time.

Jane went back to the paper and tried to read the caption under the photograph.

"Baby . . ." she read. She looked up at me, delighted with herself. "That word says, 'baby,' " she told me, pointing to it. Then she frowned and began battling with the next one.

"Sy . . . li-vie. Baby Sy-li-vie," she said doubtfully.

"Sylivie?" I said to the baby. But she took no notice.

"Sylvie . . . Sylvie," said Jane, trying again. And it was like a miracle because the baby looked around and smiled.

"Sylvie . . . Sylvie . . ." I said. It was baby Sylvie, and she stretched out her arms and cooed. She hadn't heard her name for days and days.

"I read her name," said Jane excitedly. We were both thrilled and we kept calling her name so that she turned from one to the other, getting all laughey. Then we stopped giggling and stared at one another because it was really true. We had the baby the whole country was looking for and she was worth seventeen million quid!

I looked anxiously around and that's when I saw that man again.

He was standing barefoot outside a tent a little way off talking to another man. He waved his arm in the direction of his house. I scurried out of sight behind Jane.

"What's the matter?"

"It's his paper," I hissed. I grabbed it and tried to pull it away out of sight but Sylvie had hold of it and she began to wail and hold tight to it.

Jane gathered the paper up. "You've forgotten," she said coldly. "No more taking things. No more street kid stuff. We have money, we pay our way." She thrust the paper at me. "Now you go and give it back to him."

"Give it back?" I squeaked. "He'll kill me!" He was a big bloke!

"Not if you give it back. Go on."

She hauled me out and stuck the paper in my hand. "Quick, before he sees you," she hissed.

He turned and saw me at that very moment. There was nothing for it. Jane gave me a little shove in the back and I held out the paper and began to walk toward him. He watched me as I walked right up and pushed the paper into his big hand.

"Sorry," I muttered. I began to edge away but he grabbed my sleeve. I cringed down.

The man he was talking to laughed.

The old man looked at him and blew through his beard. His eyes were wide open. "What did you give it back for?" he demanded.

I turned and gestured to Jane. "My sister told me."

The old man looked at Jane. He puffed, pushed me out of the way and went lumbering over to her. He stood there staring down at her. Jane smiled weakly at him. Sylvie began to cry as he got up close. He was huge. "What did you make him give it back for?" he demanded.

"It's yours," said Jane proudly.

"What's that got to do with it?" demanded the old man. He looked cross. "Making him give it back when he got clean away. You won't get very far like that. Giving it back!" he complained.

"But it's yours," insisted Jane.

He shook his head. "You've got no bloody sense, you kids." He turned to look at me. I'd hidden behind Jane again. "And you're not much of a thief," he told me. "Crashing about like a rhinoceros. If it'd been me stealing it you wouldn't have heard a thing."

"But you can't run like me," I cheeked him, because I could see he wasn't angry.

He shook his head and stamped his foot impatiently. "I wouldn't have *needed* to run," he told me.

Jane laughed, and he turned his wide-eyed, teasing gaze on her. "Don't you teach him anything?" he wanted to know.

"Don't go on like that," she scolded. "I want him to know not to steal things."

"I'm impressed," admitted the old man, "by how bloody stupid you are!" I laughed. "No, I mean it. If he doesn't learn how to steal around here he won't learn anything!"

He turned and waved his stick in the air, indicating everything—the poor shacks, the poor people. "Do you think anyone's going to give your things back? Look . . . he stole my paper fair and square. When you're as old as I am, you can start giving people things. Here . . ." He started rummaging in his pocket and took out a handful of change. He picked out a five-pound piece and held it out to me. "Go on, take it," he urged. I sneaked out and took it and retreated rapidly.

"Say thank you," said Jane.

"How do you know I didn't steal it?" asked the old man, twinkling at her.

We both laughed and the old man allowed himself a little smile for a second before he went wide-eyed and serious again.

"What's that?" he asked in disgust, prodding our tent with his stick.

Jane shrugged. "It'll do for now," she said apologetically.

"You mean you're going to live in it?" he asked incredulously. He sucked his beard and shook his head. "You don't know you're born, that's your trouble," he complained. "My name's Scousie." He lifted his stick again and pointed around at the camp. "Everyone knows me. Just ask for Scousie, they'll know who you mean."

"Have you lived here a long time?" asked Jane.

"I don't *need* to live somewhere a long time for people to know who I am," he said, shuffling his feet in amusement. "I'm Scousie—that's why!"

He pointed his stick at me. "You look after her, she's got no sense."

"She's my sister," I said proudly, because even though it was true that she had no sense, there was no one like my sister Jane.

Jane laughed. The old man saluted her with his stick and shuffled away. He'd gone about three yards when he turned and threw the newspaper at us. He shook his stick as if he was angry. His pale eyes wrinkled up and his great big yellow-stained, toothless mouth gaped open and he laughed, banging his stick and shuffling in amusement.

"You've got no bloody sense!" he shouted. "No more than I have!"

"Thanks!" shouted Jane. She was triumphant. It was like she

said. We'd done it right and now he was our friend. "Thanks!"

"Oh, aye," said Scousie. "Everyone knows me. You ask." And he limped away, leaning on his stick and shuffling in the mud with his bare feet.

Sham came back a little while later in a terrible temper. He had a brick with him—all he'd found in all that time. He chucked the brick down and lay on a blanket.

"Where did you get it?" I asked.

"Stole it," said Sham. I looked at Jane but even she couldn't get cross about a brick. She fitted it in among the stones holding the polythene down. Sham was staring at the baby angrily.

"We're wasting our time," he said bitterly.

"Her name's Sylvie," I told him. "Jane read it in the paper."

"But I couldn't make out any more," she admitted.

Sham made a face. "We don't know anything about her or anything. I bet it's the wrong baby, anyway," he whined. "Look at her . . ."

We looked. She was covered in mud. She didn't look like seventeen million pounds. She didn't look like tuppence.

Jane got the newspaper and showed him the photograph, but Sham wasn't impressed.

"That's not her," he insisted.

Jane and I stared from Sylvie to the photograph. Suddenly, Sham was right. They looked the same but so did all babies. One was pink and rich. Ours was a filthy brat. How could she be worth all that money . . . how could she be on TV and in the newspapers? She was just a kid, like us.

"Sylvie . . . Sylvie . . ." said Jane. But the baby was busy and didn't look up.

"See," whined Sham. "See . . ." His voice was high and he sounded as if he might start crying. He went to lie inside the tent. Jane sat there staring for a second, then she got up suddenly and walked off.

"Where are you going?" I called. But she didn't reply.

The baby began to cry. I picked up a pacifier and stuck it in her mouth.

Jane came back ten minutes later with a radio.

"The news—we can listen any time we want," she said. "Now we'll see. Now we'll get going."

She turned it on and ran the dial around and the different stations rattled past. We didn't know which ones had the news; none of us had ever bothered with the news before. We only listened to music stations on old radios we found on the Tip.

Finally she found a station with a lot of talk and we decided to leave it on that and wait. Sham had a watch—you can pick up cheap watches on the Tip anytime. We waited for the half hour to come around but there was no news. Sham fiddled with the dial again and when he went back to the talk station there it was.

"There is still no further news of baby Sylvie Tallus, who was kidnapped from her home in North London earlier this week. Ransom demands have been made and negotiations are believed to be underway . . ."

The newscaster went on to the rest of the headlines. We stared at each other.

"See? We've got the wrong one," cried Sham.

"But the photo . . ." insisted Jane.

"We've run away from Mother and it's the wrong one," said Sham, his voice beginning to whine.

The news continued.

". . . of the many groups who have so far claimed responsibility for the kidnapping, the favorite remains the Monroe Gang who have been trying lately to extend their authority north of the river. Even so, police say that as yet they have received no evidence that conclusively proves who actually holds the baby. There is speculation that the baby may be the subject of gang rivalry, or that she was herself killed in the raid, as were three of her kidnappers. It is even being suggested in some quarters that she has been abducted a second time and is being held for ransom from her original kidnappers. . . ."

"Monroe's just trying it on!" cried Jane.

"He was a Monroe," said Sham, ". . . that man. He talked about Monroe . . . he knew him. I reckon he stole the baby from Monroe. I reckon he killed those other men. . . ."

Then there was a policeman speaking, who said that until they had positive evidence of who was holding the baby they would be unable to hand over any ransom.

"We'll have to get a camera and send a photo," said Sham. He reached down and scooped the baby up. He was smiling, he believed again. He blew raspberries at Sylvie. She laughed and pulled at his face.

"Earlier today, the parents of the missing child made a plea to the kidnappers . . ." the newscaster said. Then a woman's voice came on.

"I just want to say . . ." she began. We all went very quiet because she was our baby's mother and her voice was full of tears.

"I just want to say to whoever is holding my daughter . . . to look after her and take good care of her, because we love her and miss her so much. . . ." She started crying then, and it was a moment before she could go on. "And please, please get some sort of proof to us, because we have so many different people all saying they have her and no one knows who's telling the truth. . . ." She was trying hard not to start crying again, but she couldn't help it and had to stop talking. But it was certain now that we had the right baby because Sylvie grabbed for the radio. She cried. She held the radio to her head and she cried for her mother.

"We want to cooperate but we have to know who we're dealing with," her mother said.

Then there was a man's voice. "I'd just like to add that people have to bear in mind that the very large sums of money being demanded take time to get together. We can't just go to the bank. It will take some time. . . ."

We all began talking at once. Sylvie was crying because her mother's voice had gone. Sham was saying we should go for the ransom after all, what did it matter so long as they got their baby back? Jane was wailing, "Oh, that poor woman—she must be missing her baby so much . . ." and I was arguing that we ought to tell them how much reward we wanted before we handed the baby back.

"That wouldn't be a reward, it'd be a ransom, dummy," said Jane in disgust. Then she shouted, "Oh, shut up, listen . . . !"

The newscaster was on again and we all shut up just in time to hear him say, ". . . parents of missing baby Sylvie Tallus."

"We missed the names!" groaned Jane. "How'm I supposed to get in touch if I don't even know their names, you stupid pair of kids . . . !"

But it didn't matter because now we were certain. I stared at that silly little baby and I was saying, "I don't believe it, I don't believe it . . ." I just hadn't believed it all up till then, even though I thought I had. I grabbed the baby and held her up in the air and I shouted, "You silly little thing! You silly little thing!" and she gurgled and laughed and reached out for my nose. Then Sham took her and threw her up in the air. She was laughing! She didn't know what had happened to her.

Then Jane joined in. We all threw her to each other while she shrieked and laughed and gurgled . . . all seventeen million quid of her. Then we fought over her and we ended up in a heap and almost knocked the tent down.

After a bit we calmed down and started talking properly. We decided that the gunman had been one of the Monroe Gang who'd kidnapped the baby, and then he'd tried to set out on his own and shot the others who'd helped him. But he got shot himself, and that's how we found him.

Danny Monroe would be furious.

Danny Monroe was one of the biggest gangmen in the City. You don't steal from Danny Monroe. He'd pay anything to know where the baby was and he'd kill anyone who got in his way. What was worse, we were in his territory. He controlled all the rackets in Santy. Monroe had come out of the camps himself, they said. Everyone wanted to be on his side. Maybe Mother Shelly had sold him the information Shiner brought her. Maybe he knew about us already.

Later we heard the news all over again and this time we caught what the newsman said at the end: "The magnate John Tallus and his wife Diana, parents of the missing baby."

None of us had heard of John Tallus even though the newsman said he was one of the richest people in the country. We had to listen for hours and it was quite late at night before we found out what he did. He owned television companies and newspapers. He owned the *New Dawn* newspaper which was one of the biggest. Everyone read it.

"It's easy!" said Jane. "We ring up the *New Dawn*. They'll put us in touch with him. Tomorrow," she said. "See? We nearly done it. It'll be over tomorrow!"

"There's no reward," said Sham. "They never said anything about a reward."

"There will be," said Jane. "I promise, Sham."

"We ought to tell them what we want—like Fly says," said Sham, glancing at me.

"It'll be all right," she insisted. "It'll be all right, I promise it will. All right, Sham? All right?" She was almost begging him. It was humiliating for her to beg him like that but she kept on until he said yes, just to shut her up.

He kept watching me and I knew he was waiting for me. Sham knew how these things worked, he could pull it off if anyone could. I could be in on it but I couldn't make up my mind. I didn't think he'd wait much longer.

Jane didn't notice. She really believed that she could promise things like that and that he'd believe her and that it meant something when he gave his word.

The rain began again, flicking and spattering in little bursts on the polythene. We wrapped ourselves up, me and my sister together and Sham over on the other side with the baby. We went to sleep thinking about making good, about getting out, and listening to the rain cracking on the sides of our tent.

seven

I was woken up by shouting and beating wind. I was freezing wet; it was dark. I was sitting in a pond and the rain was teeming in; the tent was heaving and shuddering in the wind and, as I watched, it tore free on one side and we were suddenly outside in the face of the storm howling at us and the driven rain. We were trying to catch hold of the thrashing sheet of wet polythene and to get our blankets out of the water and keep ourselves dry and the baby dry all at the same time. Sylvie was screaming, we were screaming. The wind was too strong. There was nowhere to run and hide and we were already drenched. We crouched down and tried to hold a corner over us but it was horrible with that sheet of wet polythene slapping and beating at us in the dark.

"Come on, you lot! Out—come on . . ."

"They've found us!" yelled Sham. We all started to run for it. I thought we were dead. But I knew the voice. It was the big old man with the Santa Claus beard—Scousie.

"What a bloody mess," he bellowed above the wind, poking our tent with his stick. "Kids! Can't even build a tent. You're coming back to mine. . . ."

We struggled through the wind toward him. It was vile. We'd have gone with anyone.

"Bring your things—no point wasting 'em," yelled Scousie over the thrashing remains of our tent. We scooped everything up in a wet tangle and splashed and slid through the mud after him.

The old man's house was a dark shape in the night. He made us take our food and blankets from the bundle and he dropped an enormous stone in the middle of the polythene to hold it against the wind. Then he pushed us inside.

There was a sweet, sour smell, close and damp. We could hear the rain splattering against the plastic windows, but the walls were so thick with layers and layers of turves and corrugated iron, and more turves and polythene, that the sound of the storm almost vanished when he pushed the door closed. In the middle was a wood-burning stove with a kettle on it.

"Don't let the baby touch it, it'll take her skin off," said Scousie.

Jane pushed back her wet hair. "Thanks," she said. Scousie waved his hand at her and she sat down and began undressing Sylvie, who suddenly began screaming her head off. Sham and I got close to the stove.

There were shelves all around covered with jars and bottles of this and that and you had to keep ducking to miss all the things hanging from the ceiling. It was a big place but there wasn't much room because it was so full. There were piles of wood for burning, a propane gas camp stove, Scousie's huge armchair, some wooden chairs, a table, and mess and rubbish everywhere. At the back was a small room almost entirely filled with a huge double mattress covered with a tangle of gray, smelly sheets.

"You get over there and get those wet things off," he ordered me and Sham, pushing us to the front door where there was a mat. He flung us a handful of towels and blankets to wrap ourselves in and got us to wring out our wet things and hang them to dry above the stove. When she'd done the baby he sent Jane into the bedroom at the back to get changed while he warmed a bottle of milk. She came back out dressed in a big, fluffy brown dressing gown and one of his old shirts.

She looked anxiously at him. "Thanks," she said again. "You saved our skins."

The old man shook his head, staring at her. "I knew that thing wouldn't last the night," he said.

"We'd have been frozen . . ." began Jane. But he waved his hand at her dismissively.

"I expect you're hungry as well," he accused. No one said anything but he took down a big frying pan from a hook and put it on the stove, and he got to work cooking an enormous meal of fried potatoes and eggs even though it was the middle of the night. Sham fed the baby her warm milk. She curled up, drank it down, and fell straight to sleep.

I hadn't realized how hungry I was. We'd been living off bread and biscuits. That old man lived in the poorest part of Santy but he had everything. There was even a little kerosene fridge in one corner. When we'd finished he made us all a big mug of milky cocoa with sugar in it. It was gorgeous.

"No, no—it doesn't cost me nothing," he insisted when Jane tried to offer him some money. "My son gets everything for me," he boasted. He puffed through his beard and poured a big belt of whiskey into his cocoa. Then he sat down in his big armchair and watched us scraping our plates clean at the dirty wooden table.

"Bloody kids," he said. "Couldn't blow a candle out on a windy day."

When I woke the next morning Jane was sitting with her legs curled underneath her on the settee sipping tea. The old man was in his huge armchair playing with Sylvie. He opened his eyes wide and winked at me, and lifted her into the air to blow bubbles on her tummy with his big, wet, beardy mouth. Sylvie gurgled and shrieked. The old man laughed, but she was half terrified.

"You're a little horror, you are," he told her.

"Scousie's been wonderful," Jane told me. "He's so good with Sy." Sham was eating cereal and cold milk from the fridge at the table. I was thinking "Who's Sy?" when he looked up at me and rolled his eyes. I got it—Scousie had wanted to know the baby's name and Jane had said Sy, which wasn't all that clever. I shrugged and went to join in breakfast.

Jane was delighted because it had worked out just as she thought things should. She was laughing and smiling and making a big fuss of everyone—getting us more cereal and milk, making Scousie tea and cutting bread for toast. Sham and I made the most of it while it lasted. We ate until we ached.

"You're so generous," she kept telling the old man. "So generous!"

"I was sorry for you, that's all," insisted Scousie. "It's all yours, you help yourselves. I don't do anything for it. That's the way I am. That's Scousie. But if it were someone else it might be completely different. . . ."

He wanted to know what we'd seen of Santy and where we'd been shopping and how much we'd paid. He was scandalized when we told him. He didn't ask any other questions but

Jane began telling him a story anyway—how we'd lost our parents in London and how they'd told us to meet them somewhere in town the next day. She kept glancing at us to check that we were following her tale. Scousie listened quietly. I saw him glance at the newspaper folded up on the side of his armchair. When she'd finished, he carried on as if she'd never said a word.

"I'm going to show you the ropes," he told us. "Because you don't know a bloody thing. First thing is to get your money back off that thief in the store. Then I'll show you who lives here and who your friends are and who your friends aren't, and how to build a camp and everything that you don't know. It may take forever," he added, shaking his big, bearded face sorrowfully. "You can stay here until you get sorted out." He waved away our thanks and carried on blowing raspberries on the baby's tummy.

While we tidied up the shack after breakfast, Scousie talked nonstop, boasting about himself. He'd been living in camp towns all his life, on and off. In between he'd done everything.

"I sailed around the world four times," he boasted. "Four times and I was never sick except when I was drunk. I wouldn't do it again, though. Boring, the sea is."

He'd been a seaman, an oilman, an engineer, a mechanic, but mostly he'd been a thief. He was very proud of it and he claimed he could steal anything. He didn't explain how it was he'd spent so much time in jail, though. To Scousie, thieving was a respectable occupation. He complained that all the young men were joining the gangs and dealing drugs when they ought to be out stealing things for their families. He hated the gangs. He said they were thugs who couldn't even shoplift if they didn't have a gun in their hands.

That reminded me what the man and the shop woman had

said to us earlier, and I asked if the Squads ever came to Santy.

"We don't get Squads out here," he said. "No one to pay 'em, is there?"

After breakfast we walked to the local store where we'd bought the stuff for our tent. The shopkeeper smiled warily when he saw we were with Scousie. A small woman with long dark hair was buying food.

"I wouldn't buy anything off him, luv—he's a thief," Scousie told her. The man laughed.

"I know," the woman said. "But so am I!" She and Scousie beamed and laughed. Then he leaned across the counter and threw the polythene at the shopkeeper.

"We want our money back," he said.

The shop man pulled disgustedly at the torn wet stuff. "These goods have been ruined. I can't offer you a refund on that," he said. "Now if you'll excuse me I have a customer to deal with. . . ."

"It's no worse than the rest of your stock," said Scousie. The man ignored him and turned to the woman.

"You're a cheap thief!" bellowed Scousie. He started waddling around the shop seizing hold of dresses and clothes hanging on the racks and flinging them about the place. "Stolen, all of it stolen. Rubbish too—you're not even a good thief, you can only steal rubbish!" he bellowed. We cringed at the back of the shop out of the way.

The shopkeeper tried to ignore it, but when Scousie started beating the potatoes with his stick, he lost his temper and tried to throw him out. He might as well have tried to throw a cow out. Scousie just stood there watching him while the man strained and heaved.

"We want our money back," he repeated. Then he walked

off, dragging the shop man after him. He began knocking pots and pans and knives and forks off the shelf with his stick.

By this time a crowd of people had gathered. They were all egging Scousie on. We hid as far away as we could because we were terrified the police would come. Oddly enough, even the shopkeeper seemed to enjoy it, because in between losing his temper he kept smiling and laughing, amused by the whole thing at his own expense.

"All right, all right!" he yelled at last. Scousie was lining his stick up at the crockery. "I'll give you a refund—this once!" The crowd roared with laughter and he beamed at them; you got the idea he'd said that "this once" lots of times. "Thirty quid," he said, going to the till.

"Sixty!" said Scousie flatly. We'd paid forty-five.

The man closed his eyes in despair. "Sixty—for that lot!" he complained.

"Look—he's shocked by his own overcharging!" shouted Scousie. He turned to us. "Sixty quid, weren't it?"

Sham and I nodded. Jane stuck her chin out, but in the end she nodded too because she didn't dare go against Scousie after all that fuss.

The shop man paid up the money to claps and cheers from the spectators. But Scousie didn't stop; he was having too much of a good time.

"Look at these apples!" he yelled when we got outside. He began taking apples out of a box by the door and throwing them to the crowd. "Full of worms—rotten. You try 'em. There's more juice in my beard! He stole these apples from Ozzie's warehouse!" he yelled at a startled passerby. The man laughed uncertainly. The shopkeeper came out of the shop and began raving and arguing again, but in the end he admitted it was all true. He gave each of us an apple to eat.

"Do me a favor, kids—shop somewhere else, will you?" he groaned. He chucked the baby under the chin and went back inside for a little cotton all-in-one for her to wear. It was secondhand, but good.

"Do you know him very well?" asked Sham as we walked away.

"Oh, aye, everybody knows me," said Scousie. "But anyway, he wouldn't dare pull one over on me because my son Sammy'd soon sort him out if he tried anything funny."

Scousie wanted to go and sort out the shop where we'd bought the clothes for Jane, but we were frightened. So he showed us around Santy instead.

I suppose we should have been dashing about making our phone call and everything. Mother Shelly would be on our trail, maybe even the Monroes. But we were having a good time and no one wanted to get back to business quite so soon. Besides, there was Scousie.

Scousie boasted all the time, but a lot of it was true. "Everyone knows me," he said, waving his stick generously in the air. Everyone did. Everywhere we went people shouted hellos or came up to talk to him.

"This is my son Hammy," he'd say. Or, "This is my daughter Jules who runs the café where we all go." I thought he must have hundreds of children, but after a bit he started introducing us as his sons and daughters and I realized he did that to everyone.

He was a really nice man. He had a good life there. I wouldn't want more than to have a life like that. He showed us where to buy things and introduced us to the shopkeepers so we'd get a good deal, as if we were going to stay forever. He was going to help us build our own house—he was getting some of his "sons" to work on it. He was even going to find jobs for us.

When he discovered that I wanted to be a baker he took us straight round to the local bakery. It was only a little shack with bread and cheap cakes laid out on tables inside. The oven was built of bricks round the back and they had to light a fire inside it to get the heat up—not like Luke's gas ovens. But it made good bread. Scousie was going to ask if I could help them there.

I got excited about it for a while. I could have made a proper life there—if it wasn't for the baby. She was having a great time, tucked away under Scousie's great smelly beard and watching everything with big, wide-open eyes. I thought she couldn't buy me anything better than the chance to learn to be a baker, even in this poor place, not for all her seventeen million pounds.

He also showed us where the Monroes hung out. It was a brick building, much better than any of the others. "They drink and gamble and have floor shows and that sort of thing," said Scousie shortly. He didn't approve.

We ended up with a visit to one of his friends. "This is our Sally," said Scousie proudly. "And she's the most marvelous person in the whole place—except for me, that is."

We sat on cushions drinking tea and milk out of chipped mugs. Sally had a baby a few months older than ours crawling around the floor, and she got out a load of old baby clothes to give us, and even an old stroller. It was a bit wobbly, but it worked. She and Jane started talking babies and to listen to my sister you'd think she'd been a mother all her life, instead of a couple of days. I didn't like it. She wasn't like my sister at that time. She was putting on a show but she never used to be anything but herself.

"Mashed potatoes and belly pork for dinner," said Scousie with relish. We bought the meat in a little house of sticks and mud. There was a table with the meat under a net to keep the flies off. It was clean and smelled nice which wasn't often the case with meat shops in Santy. Scousie bought a newspaper and when we got home he sat himself down in his armchair to read it, glasses perched on the end of his nose, his carpet slippers on, just like I'd first seen him, while we cooked dinner.

Jane was mashing the potatoes and the shack was full of the smell of frying meat. That smell! We were slavering. Freshly cooked meat was something we never had. There was cold stuff from the Tip and once or twice I'd bought myself a kebab but this was proper meat cooked in a proper frying pan. I kept touching it in the pan with my finger and licking it and Jane kept slapping me.

"They reckon that kidnapped baby is dead," said Scousie suddenly. There was a second's silence.

"No one can prove they've got her." He peered at us over his half moon glasses. "The police think she might have been killed. Or they've lost her." He looked at Sy and laughed. "The gangs'll be going mad!" he said gleefully. "They'll be turning the place upside down. Everyone'll think everyone else has her. Trouble with the gangs—they don't trust one another. They always end up tearing themselves to bits. Now, when I was a working thief, we used to cut out a window round the back, slide in, take what we wanted and slide out again. No one would know a thing about it till they found the window the next day. This lot—they kick open the door and go charging about shooting everything up and tearing the place to pieces and they call it theft. Thieves? A bunch of thugs! I just wish my boy would pack it in and get on with it on his own. Waste of a good thief!"

Scousie looked at Jane. "Didn't I tell you?" he said, all wide-eyed innocence. "My boy Sam's in with the Monroes. Oh, he's a big man. Danny Monroe doesn't do anything without asking our Sammy what he thinks. Everyone knows him around here. I keep telling him—he'll get shot up one day. He'll be around tomorrow. You'll meet him if you're about." And he peered at us again over the top of his glasses.

"We'll . . . have to go and make that phone call," said Jane. Scousie nodded and went back to reading his paper. I watched him for any sign he knew what was going on but he kept his nose in the paper and never said another word.

After we'd eaten Scousie went out. "Going for a drink," he said. "I won't be long. I don't drink like I used to," he promised, as if we knew how he used to be. He put on his hat, picked up his stick, and the door closed behind him.

"He knows," said Jane at once. I made a face. "Why did he tell us what it said in the paper, then?" she demanded. "Why did he say his son was coming tomorrow?"

Sham said nothing. He was lying on the floor, wedged in between the fridge and Scousie's big chair, playing with Sy. Jane had fed her and changed her and she was full of herself, grabbing at Sham's hair and squealing.

Jane licked her lips. She glanced from him to me. "We ought to tell him," she said.

"Tell him?" snapped Sham. He sat up and put Sy on the floor. She wailed in frustration.

"Get him on our side," said Jane quickly. "He can read and write. He's done lots of things. He'd know what to do—he'd help us. . . ."

Sham stared coldly at her. "He's a Monroe," he said.

"His son is," I said.

"Same thing."

"He told us that for own good," insisted Jane. "And he

knows anyway, I'm sure of it. We might as well."

"If he knew he'd have said," said Sham. He lay back down on the ground, picked Sy up and began tickling her toes. He shook his head. "No one would miss a chance to get in on a thing like this if they knew about it."

Jane scowled. "What do you think, Davey?" she asked me.

I liked Scousie. I trusted him. I was sure he knew. But—"I don't know, I don't know," I complained angrily. "Don't ask me. . . . Anyway, I'm fed up with the whole thing. I don't want anything to do with it. I'd be happy to stay here and help that baker. That'd do me. . . ."

"You don't mean that, do you, Davey?" said Jane. She sounded so surprised. I suppose I was being a coward. Looking back, I don't know what I wanted. I'd have loved to stay there and bake bread in that brick oven in the field. But the baby was a crock of gold.

Sham ignored me and carried on. "Why should we share the reward with him? We can do it on our own, right? Besides, I don't trust him. He's got a big mouth."

And I thought—he's up to something. Sham hadn't been idle. Why was he so sure Scousie didn't know? What right had he got to talk about trust?

"If you've got a big mouth, you don't know what's what," said Sham. And he looked up at me.

I knew what that look meant. He was giving me a last chance to come in on it with him. Sham was right and Jane was wrong but I knew at that moment I wasn't going to betray my sister for the likes of him. First her—then me. That's how it'd be. I couldn't trust Sham as far as I could spit.

"He's the one we can't trust," I said suddenly, nodding at Sham. He turned to watch me. "You don't know him," I told Jane. "No one trusts Sham. He drops people, he does everything on his own. He's up to something. We ought to—"

"I don't want to hear this," said Jane angrily. She shook her head. "Sham's part of this with us—all together. What's wrong with you?" She hated to hear things that didn't agree with her plans. But I knew Sham and she didn't.

"All together, yeah—that's why he asked me to dump you and go off with him," I said.

Sham looked at me, a real poisonous look.

"Is that true?" demanded Jane.

"Sure it's true," said Sham. "That was yesterday morning, and it's taken him this long to make up his mind."

That made me wince. It didn't seem to matter that I'd ended up sticking with her.

"I see," said Jane. She got up and began tidying up—sorting things out on the shelves, putting them in neat little piles. "Davey's made his mind up now, Sham," she said. She was trying not to cry.

I could feel Sham looking at me. I'd let both of them down. There was a long silence, filled only with Jane rattling away tidying. Sham was half sitting up, watching us both like the rat he was.

"What are you going to do?" I asked her in a minute.

"I'm not doing nothing," said Jane. She picked up a cloth and began wiping, wiping away at the clean table, at the clean shelves. "If Sham wants to betray us, I can't stop him. I'll deal with it when the time comes. But I'll tell you this." She turned to look at Sham. Her eyes were brimming over. "You give us away, you let us down a hundred times, but I won't ever let you go. If I escape you and finish this business, I'll track you down and I'll hand over your share as if you was my own brother. I'll trust you no matter what you do. I promise, I promise . . ." She was really crying now. "You remember. Okay? Okay? I promise, I promise!" she screamed.

"Okay, all right, I heard you," hissed Sham furiously. Jane sat down and she wept.

It sounded brave but what else could she do? As for Sham, he turned back and pretended to play with the baby again but I could see he was hiding his face. He was blushing, a real deep crimson blush. I didn't realize the sort of effect she was having on him. After a couple of minutes he got up and made for the door.

"Tomorrow we go into town to make that phone call," said Jane. Sham paused at the door. "All three of us," she went on. "See what's going on. Okay?" she said.

Sham nodded and ran out. Jane ran to the door after him.

"It could all be over in another day," she called.

Jane came to sit by me. I couldn't look at her. "It's all right, Davey," she said. "I know how it is. He knows it all, doesn't he? And I'm just a girl. But that's not all there is to it, see. You see how he is with Sy. He loves her. That means something." She paused and giggled. "Did you see him run out? He was crying, I think."

I hadn't seen that. Could she do that to him? If anyone had told me that my sister could make someone like Sham blush or cry I'd never have believed it. I began to wonder for the first time if Jane really could turn the whole thing around and just walk up to the parents and give them the baby back and win everything. Maybe—but not with Sham around. Sham was out there on his own and he could be up to anything. I don't know, maybe I just wanted to believe in her because I felt I'd let her down.

eight

Sham came in late, when we were getting ready for bed. We didn't ask him where he'd been and he didn't say. I don't know what time Scousie came in. He was asleep in the middle of the floor the next morning, and the whole place stank of sour booze.

There were no telephones in that part of Santy—no telephones, no electricity, no gas. You even had to buy bottled water in the shops. We were going to get a bus into London to make our call. Scousie had offered to organize a mobile phone, but we wanted to get right away from where we were staying in case they traced the call, so we told him we had to go somewhere to try and meet our parents.

Nearly all the buses from our part of Santy went by Farthing Down and we didn't dare go through there. We had to catch one bus across Santy and then another into London. We were in Sidcup before we felt far enough away.

We got off by a pub on a busy street corner and almost at

once we were sick scared. This was it. I'd never heard of anyone trying to ring up a man like John Tallus. You had the feeling bad was bound to come from it—that it was bad luck just to mention his name, even though we were only trying to do him a favor.

We walked up and down the street a few times. Sy was happy, rattling along in the stroller Sally gave us. Sham walked behind, as if the whole thing was nothing to do with him. He wasn't part of us now, not since last night. Jane was worried because we might not have enough change to put in the telephone so we went and changed some money—loads, far too much of it. Sham was looking the whole time as if he knew better, which he probably did. Then we walked up and down while Jane kept trying to decide which phone booth was the best one to call from, as if that made any difference.

"You're just scared," said Sham.

"Are you going to do it?" demanded Jane. Sham shrugged, but he didn't offer.

"Sod it, let's do it," said Jane suddenly. She turned around, walked back to the nearest booth and went in.

The first thing was to find out the number from directory assistance. It turned out there were three different *New Dawn* offices. We had no idea which one we wanted. In the end the operator gave her the head office. Then there was nothing between us and that awful call. Jane kissed me. "Wish me luck, Davey," she begged. Then she dialed the number.

We all three had our ears pressed to the receiver.

"Good morning, *New Dawn* Publications," said a woman's voice.

"Oh, hello," said Jane. "I want to talk to Mr. Tallus, please."

"Mr. Tallus is in a meeting at the moment. Can I take a message?" said the woman.

"I really want to speak to his wife. I've found his baby, I think," said Jane.

The woman said, "Just a minute, I'm putting you through."

"Please hurry," begged Jane.

"Hold on, please."

There was a pause and a man's voice said, "Hello? Can I help you?"

"Mmm—Mr. Tallus?" gasped Jane.

"I'll put you through to Mr. Tallus once we've established that you have genuine information." He sounded bored.

"I've found her. The baby. I've got her here in the telephone booth with me."

"We get a lot of phone calls about the baby," said the man. "As you may have heard, we do need some sort of identification. Is there anything you can tell us?"

"Well, she's just a baby. . . ."

"Tell him what she looks like," Sham hissed. Now it was actually happening he was right in there with us. I was glancing up and down the road because I was sure that as soon as we were put through they'd started tracking us down. Maybe they could track us down very quickly.

"She has brown eyes . . ." began Jane.

"So do a lot of babies," said the man, sighing.

"How can I prove it?" Jane begged. "She's just a baby, isn't she?"

"I'm sorry . . ." began the man.

"Well, what sort of thing, then?"

"If I told you that it wouldn't prove anything, would it?" said the man, laughing slightly.

"Come on, Jane, let's clear off. They'll be tracing our phone," I begged her. "Please . . ."

"Hang on," said Sham. Jane stuffed money into the slot

while Sham turned the baby up this way and that, trying to find something. She really was just a baby like any other baby. Then Sham remembered something. He turned her upside down. She was gurgling and screaming because she thought it was a game. Sham pulled down her diaper and there it was— a birthmark. A pale pink birthmark that had almost faded away. Jane nodded and gave Sham the thumbs-up.

"She's got a birthmark just above her bum," said Jane into the telephone. "A pale pink birthmark."

"What sort of birthmark?" asked the man sharply.

"Sort of pink—pale, like I said. Shaped a bit like a—well not like anything really—sort of oval. And pointy at one end," said Jane.

"That's it," said the man. "That's it. You have—you have— you've got her there with you?"

"Yeah, she's a lovely baby. We're taking really good care of her."

"Hold the line, please hold the line." There were some clicks. Sham was grinning and nodding. My heart was beating so hard. It had begun at last.

"Is the baby all right?" asked the man.

"She's fine, fine," insisted Jane. "We're looking—"

Then there was another click and a different voice said, "This is John Tallus speaking."

Jane gulped and gawped. She couldn't get a word out.

"Hello? Hello?" he said.

Sham nudged her. "Er . . . hello, Mr. Tallus . . ." began Jane. Then she stopped.

"You have the baby? You know about the birthmark?" demanded the man.

"Yes, we told your friend," said Jane. "She's here with us. I was just saying, she's fine, she's really well, Mr. Tallus, we're looking after her very well, Mr. Tallus. We give her whatever we can get for her and she's very happy. Here, listen . . ."

Sham had put Sylvie down and she was sitting on the floor playing with the litter and cooing and talking to herself. Jane put the telephone to her but she stopped talking and started playing with the phone instead.

"She stopped as soon as she saw the telephone, Mr. Tallus, but she's fine, honestly," said Jane.

"What do you want?" said John Tallus.

"We don't want anything—no really—we really, really don't want anything. Unless you want to. You know. We just want to give your baby back because we found her. We found that man in the cardboard boxes before he died. We're just kids, see, Mr. Tallus? We don't want a ransom. We don't want seventeen million pounds. We're just doing the right thing and we're hoping maybe you'll—that there might be a reward for finding her . . ."

"How much?" he demanded. "How much do you want?"

"I can't say, it's not a reward if we say. You have to offer it. Look—we want to do it right, see? We just want you and your wife to have your lovely little baby back. But it'd be nice if we had a reward because we got nothing. See?"

Mr. Tallus paused. "We'll issue notification of a reward through the media. Is that what you want? No ransom, a reward?"

Jane smiled like an angel at us over the telephone. "See?" she whispered. "See?"

"Say—a hundred thousand pounds?" he said.

We stared at one another. Jane put her hand over the mouthpiece. "How about that?" she demanded of Sham.

He looked shocked too. He'd never thought anyone would give away so much! He tried to shrug and look cool. "We won't be millionaires on that," he said.

"Is it enough?" asked Mr. Tallus anxiously. Maybe he heard

Sham. "People think this kind of money is just sitting there but I have to raise it."

"You don't have to give us anything if you don't want to. It's a chance for people like us to do someone like you a favor, Mr. Tallus. Street kids don't get much of a chance," babbled Jane.

"Two hundred thousand? Three hundred? Why don't you just tell me . . ."

Jane dropped the phone. She didn't mean to, she was shocked. But it cracked on the little shelf in the phone booth and dropped right on Sylvie's head. She started screaming and screaming.

"Oh, no!"

Jane scrambled after it and picked it up.

"Hello? Hello?" she said.

"What's that? Is she all right? What are you doing?" he was demanding.

"I just dropped the phone, Mr. Tallus," babbled Jane. "She's all right, Mr. Tallus, honest. She's a lovely baby. We're taking good care of her." Sham was patting her and soothing her down. I whipped a pacifier out and stuck it in. She took it and began sucking.

"It was just an accident—she's better now. I'm so sorry, Mr. Tallus."

There was silence on the other end of the phone.

Jane babbled on desperately. "You don't have to give us anything at all, honest, see Mr. Tallus." Sham glared at her and started banging her ribs with his elbow. "Not unless you really want to . . ." she added.

"Oh, I want to, I really want to," said Mr. Tallus. "I just want you to make sure Sylvie comes to no harm. I guess we understand one another."

"Oh, I hope so, Mr. Tallus."

"Tell me how she is—is she okay? Eating well and every-thing. I'm willing to pay you well to take good care of her."

I hissed. "They can find out where we are."

"Mr. Tallus, my brother says we have to go now. We have to make a date to give you back your baby. Listen, just your wife, because she's such a nice lady—I heard her on the radio. We'll meet her, all three of us, and give her her baby back. And thank you for being so generous, Mr. Tallus."

"Don't mention it."

"We just want to get off the streets, see."

"Where will you meet her?" he demanded.

Somehow we hadn't thought of that. Stupid! Jane looked desperately at us. "Where?" she hissed.

I looked out of the window. "Here," I said. "Tomorrow." I looked at the phone; the number began with 6. "Six o'clock." I wasn't thinking. I just said it. Sham stared at me, because it wasn't like me to be so quick on the uptake but I wanted to get out of there.

"Here," said Jane. "I mean . . ." She clapped her hand over the mouthpiece. "Where are we?" she demanded.

"Sidcup, innit?" said Sham.

I opened the door of the booth and called to a man walk-ing up the road. "What road is this, mister?" I begged.

He glanced up at the road sign—there was one right by us on the wall.

"North Cray Road," he said.

Jane nodded. "North Cray Road, Sidcup. By the phone booth . . ." she began.

But Sham suddenly leaned across and grabbed the phone, stopping the mouthpiece with his hand. "You only bloody told him where we are," he hissed fiercely. He dropped the phone and glanced down the road.

"Oh, God . . ." groaned Jane.

"Wait a minute," said the man.

Jane snatched the receiver which was dangling down on its cord.

"At six o'clock tomorrow night," said Jane. "Your wife, her that was on the radio."

Then she slammed down the phone and we legged it. He only had to ring up the police and they'd be there! I bet he was on the phone that same second. We were certain we'd had it, but we managed to jump on a bus. It was going the wrong way—into town I mean, but it got us away. We got off a little later and caught another one—and then another one—just going anywhere to break our trail. Only then did we start looking for buses to take us back.

Once we felt safe, we started grinning. We just kept looking at each other and grinning because we'd done such a thing! He was going to give us our fortunes. We were rich! Tomorrow evening, we could start to live.

"That much money must be just peanuts for that guy!" I said wonderingly.

Jane kept leaning across and whispering, "See, I told you, I told you!"

I'd never felt so proud of my sister. She'd been right all along! I'd thought she was just a stupid girl but she'd rung up someone like John Tallus. She'd done it, she'd done it her way, a way no one would ever have dreamed. She'd been the only one who'd known what making good really meant and now she'd done it and I'd done it with her, and we were going to make it. I felt I was rich already! Sham was celebrating too to start off with, but after a bit he got all superior and thoughtful again and sat there watching us as if we were a pair of kids.

I suppose it was seeing him being so cool that set me thinking. About halfway back my brain started working. We'd done it all wrong! They had a whole day to get ready for us. We'd never get anywhere near that telephone booth! I turned around to look at Sham, sitting there like Mr. Wise Guy on his own. He knew, he'd known all along. He was smart. He must have been laughing at us for a couple of dopes the whole time.

I had to keep quiet on the bus but when we had to change to get the bus into Santy, I dragged Jane up into the doorway of a derelict shop.

"We'll never get anywhere near," I hissed. "They'll have the place staked out. As soon as we get off the bus they'll grab us and take Sy off us. We've been stupid. . . ."

"Why?" said Jane. She seemed really puzzled. "We're going to give her back anyway. . . ."

I shook her arm. "It's a trick. Why should he believe us?"

She scowled. "Why shouldn't he believe us?"

"We should have found somewhere and made them come to us. We shouldn't have given them any time," I said.

"I told him we wanted to do it right," insisted Jane.

"We don't mean anything to them. We're just street kids," I moaned. "You shouldn't have told him we were street kids." I watched as Sham came sauntering up. He had it all worked out.

"You knew," I spat at him.

Sham looked mildly surprised. "What's the problem? One of us keeps the baby and they only get it back after we've got our reward. Right, Jane?" he said brightly.

Jane said, "It wouldn't be a reward, then, would it?" between her teeth. "I promised. I said I'd give her her baby back."

Sham shrugged as if it meant nothing. "You're in charge," he told her. He was looking at me. I couldn't say anything I was so furious.

"Mr. Tallus is a good man," insisted Jane. "He has so much. What does he need to do things like that for?"

"Why should he pay a reward to get his own baby back?" I argued. "We're rubbish kids. You wouldn't trust your baby to a bunch of rubbish kids, would you?"

"Don't think like that," she scolded. People were beginning to watch us. She looked at me unhappily. "We'll talk about it later."

I was sick. I knew I was right and I knew why Sham wasn't backing me up, too. He had it all worked out. I didn't know what it was, but I was pretty sure I'd soon find out. I started up again as soon as we got off the bus in Santy.

"He's going to betray us," I told Jane. "He already has. We should clear off quick—you and me. Leave him to it."

"He's one of us," said Jane coldly. Sham just stood there, plain-faced, as if we were talking about the weather.

"You git," I told him.

Jane blew up. "Listen, Fly Pie," she hissed. She was furious. "In the first place, I don't care if we do get jumped tomorrow. We done it the best way we could. We'll get a chance to say our piece, we'll tell 'em what we are and what we done. If they want to do us after that, what does that make them?"

"You're mad!" I screamed. "What does it make us? What do you think they'll do? Haul us up in front of the court, a bunch of rubbish kids? They don't need to do that."

"They can do what they want," she insisted. "And in the second place, Sham can stab me in the back till his arm drops off. I'm not going to stop trusting him or you, or Mr. Tallus or anybody. So stuff that in your pipe and smoke it!" And she tossed her head and stormed off, shoving the stroller through the rutted mud and leaving me and Sham standing there together.

Sham watched her rattle furiously off. "She's bonkers," he said, with some awe.

She really was bonkers. She'd let them slit her throat—and mine too—rather than give us a decent chance. I don't know if she'd always been like that and I'd just never noticed, or if being sold on as a prossie had done something to her or what. I couldn't be expected to go along with this, it wasn't reasonable. It wasn't *right*.

I eyed Sham up and waited. He dug his toe in the mud.

"I'm going for a walk," he said. He nodded his head at Santy, as if he was going everywhere and anywhere. "See you back there."

I watched him sidle away between the shacks and sheds. I wished I was going with him. He was gone over three hours.

nine

It was a windy night again. Scousie shut up his home. He bolted the door, shuttered the windows, stuffed rags and paper in the cracks to keep the draft out. He fired up the stove until it roared and we settled down to pass the night.

It was a funny atmosphere. We didn't ask Scousie about his son, he didn't ask us about our trip to town and we didn't ask Sham where he'd been. It was a day that had never been. After the dishes were washed and the baby asleep Scousie sighed and pulled out a pack of cards.

"I'll show you how to play poker," he said.

"What stakes?" asked Sham.

"No, no, no, just for matchsticks. I never bet, not on the dogs or the horses or anything. Why should I pay the bookie's wage, he doesn't pay mine. No, no, but it's a good game. . . ."

It was a good game, too. Scousie kept winning and losing fortunes in matchsticks. Jane kept steadily building her pile up, fondling a bent penny all the time which she thought brought her good luck. Sham played cautiously for a while but he couldn't seem to concentrate and in the end he went to sit on the settee to watch. I couldn't get the hang of it. Scousie always knew when I had good cards and bluffed me away. It was driving me crazy. I'd faced him down at last and won a huge quantity of matchsticks when there was a knock at the door.

Scousie moved back in his chair and watched us over his half-moon spectacles. "Who is it?" he called.

"It's me, Dad."

"Our Sammy . . ." he mouthed. He waved his hand toward the bedroom and we melted away, picking up our bits and pieces on the way. Scousie lumbered slowly to the door pointing out things we'd forgotten. Diapers, the stroller, a pacifier by the chair.

"Coming, Sam . . ."

We got into the bedroom and closed the door. Jane went to the window. We all knew. I pushed a chair quietly against the door handle. Sham stood uncertainly, watching us. Then he ran to his coat and started going through the pockets.

The gun.

"You do it," I said. "You do. You do." The front door opened.

"Have you brought your friends, Sammy?" said Scousie. I pressed my eye to a crack. Three men pushed into the room. Jane tugged at the window but it wouldn't budge.

"What is it, Sammy?" asked Scousie. He had his back to us. The man he called Sammy—his son—pushed toward the bedroom but Scousie barred the way.

"What's going on?" he demanded.

Jane was heaving but the window was stuck. "Sham, help me," she hissed. Sham was frantically going through his things. He glanced at her and at the door. He was patting his coat, searching on the floor. I ran to help Jane but we were frightened of making a noise. Now Sham gave up his search and glared poisonously at us.

"Who stole it?" he hissed.

"Sham . . ." Jane groaned. We gave a great pull and the window shot open with a crack.

"Move, Dad, move!" screamed Sammy.

"Where are they?" yelled one of the other men. There was a smash of crockery.

"You stay away—" began Scousie. Then, a violent thud. I heard Scousie gasp. He'd been hit.

"Sammy," said Scousie. "Sammy . . ."

Jane was half out trying to hold a hand over the baby's mouth but Sy struggled free and screamed—a quick loud scream. The men were battering at the door. Sham made a dive for us but he lunged as if he didn't really care and I knocked him down. The door splintered. I jumped out of the window after Jane. Sham was crawling out after me. I heard the door burst open and we were running, running, the two of us skidding and running in the mud and the dark wind with Sy screaming like a witch.

Scousie was shouting. "Those three men! Help! Stop those three men!" They must have clobbered him then because he shut up. But there were people in the dark with us, crawling from tents, opening doors.

A man loomed up in front of us, his long hair beating his face in the wind. "What's going on?" he demanded.

"They're getting Scousie," gasped Jane. He dashed behind us. Other men were running to help Scousie. We were running away, we were free in the sudden crowd. But Jane grabbed my hand and dragged me to a standstill.

"Where's Sham?" she gasped.

I jerked my hand over my shoulder and made off again.

the baby and fly pie
115

Everyone was running back to Scousie's. We were safe! But Jane held my hand and stared back at the gathering crowd.

"Jane, come on!" I screamed. But she'd made up her mind. She thrust the baby into my arms. I pulled her but she shook me off. "Jane!" I bellowed. I was furious! I stared for a second and then ran after her.

Scousie's house was a blaze of light. There was a crowd around it and from inside came shouting and thumps and thuds. Everyone knew Scousie—everyone helped. Those three men didn't stand a chance. Once there was a gunshot and the crowd froze into silence. Then Scousie, bellowing like a bull: "Typical bloody gangland! Couldn't organize beer out of a bottle!" They all laughed and began shouting again.

Jane ran around the edges of the crowd. I stuck to her heels. I don't know what I'd have done if I'd found him first. He was hanging at the back of the crowd, edging to and fro, watching the wreckage of his great plan.

Jane ran up behind him and grabbed his arm. He turned and I think he nearly died of fright.

"I told you I wouldn't let you go, didn't I?" she yelled triumphantly. "I told you. I keep my word." She took hold of his hand and pulled. "Now run," she ordered.

Sham stood stock-still. His face was like a mask, so white and motionless. "Three hundred thousand!" Jane screamed at him "Three hundred thousand quid!" People were watching when she said that, but it turned Sham back to life. Woodenly he began to shamble after her and then to run. The baby was screaming and so were other people. There was shouting back there, crashes, violence.

We ran and we ran. People were still passing and a couple of times we lost one another but whenever we did we stopped and called and found each other again. Even Sham.

We carried on running until we left everything behind—the people, the fighting, the shacks and sheds. We came to a field with broken buildings in it. We were frightened of going into the buildings and we dived under a hedge instead.

We could hear shouting a way off, gusting in the wind. There were a couple more shots. We dug ourselves into the damp leaves under the hedge. Sy had stopped yelling but whimpered and whined. Jane kept sticking a pacifier into her mouth but she sucked nervously a few times and spat it back out.

We were safe. But for how long?

"He did it," said Sham. I could hardly see him in the dark. "The old man. He gave us away to his son."

"You liar," I hissed furiously. "He didn't tell, he saved us. You told on us."

"It weren't me," said Sham, his voice high.

"You lie," I said. He couldn't even be honest then. "You couldn't find the gun, that's all," I yelled. I jumped at him. I wanted to hurt him. Jane didn't stop me. I punched and kicked and he didn't try and stop me at first. But when I hurt him he began to fight back, crying in a thin voice, "It wasn't me, it wasn't me . . ."

"Leave him," said Jane after a bit.

"I told you, I told you what he was like," I cried.

"I don't care."

Sham rolled over onto his stomach, all curled up. "You see, you think I did it, too," he gasped.

I couldn't see her in the dark but she was furious. She bent down over his back that he had turned to us. "You gave us away. You went to the Monroes and you gave us away. Scousie took that gun. He saved us and you try to blame him for what you did. And I'll tell you something else—I'm still going to trust you. What do you think of that, Sly Sham?"

Sham didn't reply.

Jane turned to me. She was panting. "We'll separate," she said. "They'll be looking for us three and a baby. The Monroes. I'll take the baby, she might be mine. You two make your own way. Listen—I'll meet you—not tomorrow, the morning after. Where?"

"Not in Santy," I said.

"Luke's," she said. "The baker, your friend, okay?"

"Okay," I said, although it was a bad place.

Jane bent down and kissed me fiercely. "Here." She rummaged in her pockets and gave me a handful of money. "Look after yourself. Make sure you get there. And look after him, okay?" She gestured toward Sham lying in the dirt.

I stared at him. I didn't promise anything.

"Sham—you look after my brother like I looked after you."

Sham sniffed. He nodded into the mud. Jane crawled out of the hedge. He started crying as she ran away from us across the wet grass.

I sat listening to the wind in the branches and Sham weeping. He stayed toppled over in the dirt under the hedge. It was cold and damp. "I'm going over there," I said, pointing to one of the broken buildings. Sham didn't look at me. I left him. I found a dry corner out of the wind and some old paper sacks and I tried to make what bed I could. I was wearing my thick sweater but it wasn't enough for the night. I hoped Sham would crawl off even if it was back to the Monroes. But he turned up in a little while. He came around the side of the wall and sat down a few yards away.

He said, "You should have just run."

"I would have," I said.

He didn't reply. He fidgeted around for a bit and then he

said, "It wasn't dangerous, though. Those men were getting beat up, they couldn't do anything."

"She didn't have to go back," I said.

I felt sorry for him. I mean, he had everything going for him. He was clever and quick, he could keep on thinking when things were getting hot. He didn't trust anyone and he didn't let anyone trust him. He was streetwise. And Jane—she didn't have anything except this crazy idea she didn't even know how to pull off properly. All she could do was trust him but she used it like a weapon and Sham didn't know how to cope with that.

A bit later he said, "I didn't do it." That made me mad.

I just said, "Go to sleep." He did as I said. He crawled up into a ball and tried to go to sleep where he was. I put some of my litter over him and he stirred slightly. Then I tried to sleep, too.

ten

I woke up freezing cold. Sham was sitting against the wall and the dawn had just begun. I hadn't thought what to do, but now I was getting frightened again. We were still in Monroe land. They'd be out looking for us. Cautiously I got up and peered over the broken walls and rubble. I thought I might see the shapes of men coming across the fields toward us but there was only the long wet grass, the hedgerows, an abandoned car at the edge of the field.

"I'm going," I said. I glanced at Sham. He watched me as I climbed a heap of rubble and looked out the other way, away from Santy. There was no one there.

"Take me with you," he said.

"Only because she said."

Sham nodded and followed me out of the building. We found a plastic barrel half full of dark water and we washed in it. We were covered in mud. Sham dabbed feebly at himself and it made me hate him more because he was so weak. Then we set off across the fields. We walked a long time and it slowly began to get light.

We didn't talk. After the fright and the gunfire, after the chase and the violence, the early morning was as still and quiet as if nothing had ever happened. Everything had stopped and only we were moving on the earth. I'd never been in the country before. The birds began to sing, just a few at first, but then more and more and I thought the noise would never stop it got so loud. All the birds on earth were singing but nothing moved. It was another world. I forgot about Sham. I forgot about the baby, the kidnapping, Jane. It seemed they were singing just for me but I couldn't see them—just a black bird flicking past between the hedgerows, just a brown bird peeping at us from a branch. It was magic. I thought that nothing could happen to us while it was like that.

The sun came slowly up and it got brighter and warmer. Movement began in the hedges and grass. You got the feeling that the world was beginning and that it was getting dangerous again. I began to look around and notice things—spiders hanging in their webs, berries going black, leaves and stems and flowers. I think people who live in the countryside are lucky and I can't understand why so many of them come to live in London where it's dirty and exhausting and full of people.

There was a footpath running along behind the hedge but it began to double back toward Santy. We had a problem because two boys wandering around out here beyond the camps would attract attention. In Santy we would be less obvious but if anyone spotted us we were dead.

"What shall we do?" I asked. Sham shook his head. I was confused. I was used to leaving decisions to Jane—or to Sham.

I couldn't make up my mind and I began to wander backward and forward, trying to think.

Sham said, "We could stay outside for a few miles while it's still quiet. Then we'll be out of Monroe land and we can go back into Santy and hide. Monroe land only goes a few miles west of here."

"How do you know?"

"Someone told me," he muttered, looking away. And I thought, yes, they told you yesterday when you were talking with the Monroes.

That cleared my mind. We carried on skirting around. I had no intention of going back into Santy now. I thought we'd carry on walking for a while, because he was probably right about where Monroe land ended. Then we'd find somewhere to hide. We could catch a bus right through Santy at night into town and hide out there until we had to meet Jane. The city was full of kids. We'd just have to take our chance with them and the Squads. There was no way I was going with Sham into Santy in daylight but I didn't tell him that. The less he knew, the better.

When we came to a little village we went in to buy food. It was probably a mistake. People don't welcome Santy kids. Their village was right on the edge of the camps and in a few years it'd be swallowed up and turned from a pretty little place with gardens and trees into a muddy desert. The shopkeeper treated us like dirt but he let us buy bread and a jar of jam when we showed him our money. Then we beat it. We found a wood and crept under the wire. The trees were small and close together and inside we found some little shelters, just open huts with a bench inside.

"We'll stay here," I told Sham. "After dark we can catch

melvin burgess

a bus into town. We can hide overnight until it's time to meet Jane."

Sham nodded okay. Then we ate our bread.

That wood was a good place to hide. It was dense and there were twigs on the ground. We'd have heard someone coming before they saw us.

After a while we left the shelters and went into the thickets. We were lucky, no one came. It didn't rain either—just a few spots in the afternoon, and they hardly got through the thick trees.

It was a time of waiting again. Nothing to do but think. I wondered if Jane was still alive. Then I remembered that tonight she was supposed to be meeting Diana Tallus and I thought, "Tonight, she'll be dead or rich." I wanted to say that, but there was only Sham and I wouldn't talk with him.

A couple of times Sham got up and went away and I hoped he wouldn't come back but he did. Although I promised myself not to talk to him, it got so boring that when he asked me what I was going to do with my share of the money, I couldn't resist it. I said, "You first."

Sham said, "I'd like a big house with lots of people working for me. I want to have lots of good rackets going and make money and pay people to do things for me. Everything for me. But I don't think the reward will be enough for that so I'll have to work for a while at it."

"Perhaps Tallus'll give you a job," I said.

Sham shook his head. "I don't want a job." He said that since John Tallus was so rich, he must have a lot of rackets going and maybe he'd put Sham in charge of one. "Then I could work my way up and get more and more rackets until I was as rich as he was," he finished. He smiled at his own greed.

To be as rich as John Tallus! He wanted so much. Then he asked me what I was going to do.

"I want to buy a big baker's shop," I told him. "A big shop in the center of town that sells fancy cakes and pastries to rich people. I'd give Luke a job making bread for me, because he makes the best bread, and I'd make the pastries. Maybe Tallus'll get the gangs to leave me alone so I could just get on with it."

Sham laughed. "But that's work," he said. "You don't want to work if you have money!"

"Rackets is work," I pointed out.

Sham shook his head. "Rackets aren't work," he insisted. "I don't want to work—not me." He smiled and shook his head.

"Are you going to have children?" I asked.

Sham made a face. "Kids are trouble," he said.

"I'll have kids," I said, "and I'll send them to school and feed 'em up till they're big and fat!"

He laughed and shook his head again. "You're crazy," he said. "You've spent too much time with your sister, Fly."

We smiled at each other. Neither of us could understand how someone like my sister had managed to hijack this whole operation. Then I remembered what she'd said about how it meant something that he loved the baby.

I asked him, "What's it like having a family?"

Sham looked at the trees and said, "It's no better than anything else. I only had a mum and a baby brother, anyway. My mum was so busy so I had to look after our baby. It was a lot of work." He grinned. "I told you—I don't like work."

I grinned back.

"She used to get cross," he went on, digging in the dirt with his finger. "She used to hit me—and the baby . . ." He glanced up at me. "I used to go on the street with him—you know?" I nodded. We'd all seen boys and girls with their baby brothers and sisters on their hips in the street. "But one day I went back and my mother didn't turn up again."

"What happened to the baby?" I asked.

"He got ill," said Sham. "I took him to the hospital but they said it wasn't any good. He died, anyway. It's not much different from anything else," he repeated.

I was disappointed. Whenever I hear someone talk about families I want them to be happy and love one another, even though I know that some street kids have parents and no one loves them. But I couldn't imagine Sham looking after his little baby brother like Jane had looked after me, and hiding him from his mother who got cross.

A bit after that Sham got up and moved away.

"Where are you going?" I demanded.

"Where do you think?" he said. I stared at him for a minute, then he farted. We grinned at one another and he went off into the woods.

I didn't like it. As soon as he said it, I didn't like it, but I could hardly go with him, could I? So I sat there feeling like an idiot, because he knew I couldn't go with him and he could do whatever he wanted.

After ten minutes I started pacing around. I called him—not too loud in case someone was near—"Sham? Sham?" But there was no answer. My heart started going then. It was so typical. I went off the way he'd gone to look for him but there was nothing. I called again and when he didn't answer, I was positive. I began running around. I was scared silly. I knew it would happen, I knew it! One minute we were talking about what we'd do with the reward money and the next he was off to give us up. He could be anywhere by now. Tomorrow morning the Monroes would be at Luke's place and they'd have the baby. I was so sick and so scared and so furious I just started screaming, "Sham! Sham!" I started crying then because I was so helpless and I was screaming for him when there was a noise right near me.

And there he was.

He looked me right in the eye and said, "You want to keep your gob shut, do you want us to get caught?"

"Where've you been?"

"Told you."

"It don't take that long to have a crap," I hissed. "Did you find your friends? Or are you going to leave it till later?"

"I don't need to do that," he said.

"Oh, yeah. What's the plan then? They're going to be there tomorrow, aren't they? What are they going to pay you? Made it worth your while, did they? How much? How much?"

"Don't be an idiot, Fly, I've only been gone fifteen minutes."

"Why didn't you answer me, then?"

He scratched his head and didn't answer. He just said, "I've been thinking. I've been thinking maybe she can pull it off after all."

"Sure!" I sneered. "She's going to walk up to them and they're going to give her whatever she asks for because they like her. Don't give me that, you only came because I was shouting so loud. Figured you'd have a better chance later on, didn't you? Didn't you?" I yelled.

Sham glanced around. He picked up a stick. I took a step back but he just stood there tapping a tree with it and chewing his lip.

"So you don't think she can, then?" he said. "But I do."

I found myself a nice fat stick and got ready. I was watching him like a hawk. As soon as he made a move . . . I don't know what I was going to do to him—break his legs if I could, I suppose.

"No one's going to give anything to the likes of me or you," said Sham. "But she's different." He glanced at me to see if I was listening. "I've been thinking about it, see. You couldn't let someone like that down—"

"You did."

Sham shook his head irritably. "It doesn't matter what I did. Look—she believed I did it but she came back anyhow, didn't she? So I couldn't do it again—no one could do it now, not twice—not after that."

"You did it, though, didn't you?"

"Bloody no—listen . . ." I didn't want to listen. Why couldn't he just admit it if he wanted me to believe him? But he never would. He leaned forward, hurrying on. "If she makes me believe her, she can make them believe her. See what I mean? All they have to do is believe her. She's like she is no matter what anyone does. She can convince them. She convinced me. If I believe her—see what I mean? She can do it. No one else could, but she can."

I began to see what he meant. I was staring at him trying to work out if it was another one of his tricks, but it didn't sound like the sort of thing you just think up.

"She's the sort of person they give rewards to," explained Sham.

I was still angry with him for making me so scared. But what he said was true. It didn't matter that she was stupid and didn't know what people were like and how things worked. It didn't matter how much of a mess she made of it. If she made people different, if she made them trust her, they might reward her after all. And you had to trust Jane, anyone could see that. Even Sham trusted Jane.

the baby and fly pie
127

"Do you reckon?" I asked. I almost said "please" because I wanted it to be like that so badly and it all seemed to depend on Sham believing in her.

Sham was trying, you could see it. He was convincing himself at the same time. "No one could do it again. If I had done it, I couldn't do it again, I really couldn't. She just has to meet them and they'll see. They'll trust her. She's too . . . she's too . . ."

"Too honest! Too stupid!" I cried. I was almost doing a dance because for the first time I began to see how it could work. It didn't matter how stupid she was. If she made a couple of rubbish kids like us believe her . . .

"Too bloody good!" grinned Sham.

It was crazy, but why not? She'd got away with it so far. "You reckon? Really?" I begged.

"Sure! I couldn't do her down, not after she came back," insisted Sham. We grinned. He believed in her—Sly Sham the pickpocket, the smart guy. It was ridiculous!

I began to laugh. "She can do it!"

"Sure she can!" laughed Sham. "She's our—our secret weapon!"

And we began to laugh and laugh, because all those people looking out for us—Mother, the police, the gangs, Mr. and Mrs. Tallus—they'd be looking out for all the tricks they knew. But they wouldn't be expecting Jane!

That's what Sham said to me in the woods that day. Looking back I don't know if he believed it himself or not. You could never tell with Sham. Maybe he said it to find a way of getting me to trust him. Maybe he was on his way out to the Monroes when he heard me yelling and got scared. He never did tell me why he never answered my calls. I don't know anymore, but I believed it then—every word. After that everything was different because I knew at last that we really could do it just like she said. I was so grateful. I could have forgiven him anything for being on the same side as Jane.

We were looking forward to getting back into town but we were scared as soon as we got off the bus. It wasn't our land. We were in Clapham just because the bus went there. It was late. Soon people would be leaving the streets. The Squads worked at night. The local kids knew where to go and hide but we were strangers. Kids were dangerous, too. Even though they have nothing, the kids guard their streets like proud soldiers. Strange kids had to answer to them and you might have to join their gangs and swear oaths.

We got off the bus and heard music and we headed toward that. Where there's music there's people and where there's people there's safety. There was a big field ahead full of lights and noise and voices. People were streaming toward it. Sham and I grinned at each other. No one was going to notice two new faces in this crowd. We were together, we were friends again, better friends than we had been before. What better place to spend our time? It didn't matter that Sham had given us away—in fact it was a good thing, because if he hadn't given us away he'd never have come to believe that Jane could do it.

It wasn't a little street fair—it was a great big fair with rides. They had the Big Wheel, the Tilter, the Spinner, the roller coaster, the Cage of Death. We walked around for a bit, just staring at it like poor kids do. Then I remembered I had all that money Jane had given me in my pocket.

"I got eighty quid," I said suddenly to Sham.

"All that?" he said. He licked his lips and looked around him at all the fun and good things. He began to smile. I felt a big fat grin spreading over my face, too.

"We can get some decent clothes and somewhere to sleep for the night," I said. That was the sort of thing Jane would say.

"Yeah—yeah . . ." said Sham. We were both looking around at all the things we'd seen so often, but we'd only ever just tasted—just enough to want lots more.

"We could get a proper meal or something," I added.

"Roast chicken," said Sham, slobbering. "Popcorn. Fish-on-sticks. Burgers."

"Kebabs. Ice cream," I agreed.

Sham screamed. "Look!" he screamed. "Look—WhipSpin!"

We'd turned under the Big Wheel and we were face to face with it: "WhipSpin!" screamed Sham again. And we forgot about the somewhere-to-sleep and even the chicken and fish-on-sticks and we ran up and paid our money. The man poked it with his finger and smiled and let us into one of the little cells in the big tube. We had to wait for ages for it to get filled up and everyone noticed us, because poor kids don't have enough money for a treat like that very often. They were all smiling at us. We were so excited and out of our senses that we didn't care. We were proud!

At last the cells were all full up and we got sucked up like juice up a straw.

Have you even been on a WhipSpin? It costs the earth because it's so special and we never dreamt about having a go. Here we were, doing it with the rich kids! It's all made of clear stuff and as you get sucked up there's nothing between you and the ground. You go up hundreds of feet! You can hardly move a muscle because the cell is so tight and you can see everything under you—the Big Wheel under you, the roller coaster zipping up and down under you—everything underneath you. Sham and I were screaming and howling even though we were only still going up.

Then we got to the first loop and POP! we were spat out and went hurtling through the air so fast I could feel my stomach and even my toes dragging miles behind. We got up, up to the end of the loop and WHIPSPIN! The whole cell whips around and spins like a top and if your head wasn't held so tight inside the cell you'd break your neck. Then you speed up off in the other direction. Whack! All the way to the end of the arm. And WHIPSPIN!—and then you're hurtling down so fast you think you'll make a hole in the ground three yards deep. And WHIPSPIN!—inches from the ground and off you go, up, up, up, for another ride . . .

Sham and I got off giggling and swaying and staggering about. We had no sense left at all. After a ride there's a little compound where you can stay for five minutes to get your wits back. You can see the other people in the bottom loop just above the ground. WhipSpin!—their faces get all stretched out and they're howling and laughing all at the same time. They look funny! Then we had another go and Sham wanted to do it again, but I was sick with it and he didn't want to do it on his own. So we had a go on the roller coaster instead, and then the Mouse, and then the Cage of Death and I don't know what else. But it was all pretty tame after the WhipSpin.

After that we got thirsty so we bought some pop and we sat down on the grass to drink it. The pop was seething in my stomach. We went for a walk to see what we wanted next. We were drunk on rides! A hot smell came wafting past us.

"Roast chicken," Sham reminded me. We started slobbering again just at the thought. There was a stall selling spit chickens just by us.

All that money—we could have everything we wanted! It was as if it was all free. I bought a whole roast chicken and we sat down a few yards away from the stall and scarfed it. Then we bought another one but we couldn't eat much of it so we wrapped it up in paper and took it along for later.

"Another WhipSpin?" suggested Sham, with a greasy grin. I groaned; it would have been a disaster. We were so full! But we were so high on money we didn't dream of stopping. We had more rides—the Ghost Train, the Spinner, the High Drop, the Snake. I was sick behind a stall and then I felt like another WhipSpin. We did that and then I was hungry again so I ate a bit more chicken and then we bought two of those sugar lollies. Not the little ones—the huge ones with about ten different colors in spirals as big as your face. And we walked around slurping and licking and watching the kids stare at us and making faces—that's how far gone we were.

Two poor kids spending money like that. Walking around eating lollies bigger than our heads—and making faces at the other kids! We were asking for it.

"Those are our lollies," someone said suddenly.

There was a group in front of us—seven or eight kids, some smaller, some older than us.

"Where'd you get all that money?" one demanded.

"We've been watching you," said a girl resentfully.

"We're having a day out—our mum and dad are here somewhere," said Sham.

"You stole that money," said one of the bigger boys. "This is our patch."

"Run," said Sham quietly, pushing me away with his hand. I turned and fled.

We were weaving through the crowd, but the kids were right on our heels. There were people everywhere, we were banging into everyone. We flung our lollies behind us and some of the younger ones stopped to fight over them; then the chicken went and that stopped some more, but the bigger ones knew we had money.

Sham could run like the wind and he was ahead. I thought I'd had it. But then he fell back to my side and panted, "See you by the bus stop." And he fell down.

I couldn't believe he'd done it on purpose. I couldn't believe he'd done it for me. But there he was, rolling on the grass, and the boys were on him. I put my head down and ran fast. They were kicking and punching him but they stopped chasing me and I got clean away among the crowd and the noise and the lights.

I ran and ran. That chicken inside me didn't stop me running. I didn't want to turn a corner and come across those kids again. I passed the subway station on the other side of the road and got lost in the network of little streets behind it. Then I slowed down and I began to make my way back to the bus stop we'd got off at.

Sham wasn't there. I had to spend an hour wandering around on my own. I stayed in the streets around the fair even though I was scared of that gang of kids, because it was late now and they were the only streets with many people. I didn't want to be alone. All those kids making pests of themselves at the fair with no money to spend—it was the right sort of place for a cleanup.

I started getting scared on my own then and I thought— it's a trick. Sham's done it again, he's gone to get someone, they'll be waiting for me. . . .

I turned right around. I wanted to put as much distance between me and Sham and that bus stop as I could. But even as I ran I doubted. Why should he go now, when there was still everything to play for? So I crept back one more time and there he was. He was a mess. He had a bloody nose and a fat lip and his hair was all over the place, and his clothes were torn.

"They followed me. I had to go miles to lose them," he said. He wanted to get away from the area because they were still looking for us, so we walked quickly off.

I said, "Thanks."

"Is the money all right?" Sham asked.

"Oh . . . yes . . ." And I laughed out loud, because it wasn't me, of course, it was the money he was saving. If the kids had got me they'd have got our money. It was just common sense!

Sham's face broke into a wide smile. "They kicked hell out of me," he said proudly. "How much have we got left?"

We huddled in a doorway and counted. Twenty pounds.

"We spent sixty pounds on the fair," said Sham, in awe. "Sixty pounds!" We smiled at each other, full of pride and shock at what we'd done.

"That was the most fun I've ever had," said Sham fervently. "Even getting chased. Even getting beat up. The best!"

"We've been stupid," I told Sham. We'd spent our time enjoying ourselves and now we didn't even have anything to cover us up at night!

Sham said, "We'll manage." He wasn't bothered. Maybe it was worth it after all, but I didn't fancy another night like the last one.

We walked aimlessly around, keeping out of sight. We saw a scruffy little kid hurrying nervously down the dark roads.

"Give us a fiver," Sham said to me.

"What for?"

"Watch," he hissed. I dug out a five-pound piece and gave it to him. Sham swaggered up and stopped the kid. "Hey," he said. "Me and my friend want to know where the kids sleep at night around here. I mean the good places."

The boy glanced shiftily up the road, but he knew better than to run.

"I dunno . . ." he began, but Sham waved his hand.

"You're a street kid. You're a skinny piece of nothing. You know all right. Come on—tell us and we won't hurt you."

"We don't say where we go," the boy whined.

Sham pulled the fiver out of his pocket and held it out.

"Do you want this?" he asked.

I laughed; the boy goggled. What was a scruff like Sham doing with fivers? "Yeah, I want it," he confessed, trying not to look at it too hard.

"Tell us," said Sham.

"We go in the underpass by the Common," said the kid quickly. Sham handed over the money.

"Even better—you can take us there," he said.

The boy was willing to do almost anything on the chance there'd be more fivers. He led the way, fondling his money and watching us curiously.

"You're stupid," I whispered to Sham.

"I found out where to go, didn't I?" he boasted.

"Yeah, and he'll tell every other kid who sleeps there that we've got money to give away. We can't go there now . . ."

Sham made a face then. He'd only wanted to act the big man.

"I'll get our money back," he said.

I laughed. Just like Sham! "Let him have it, why not?" I said. "There's plenty more. Jane'll have something for us tomorrow. . . ."

"Either that or nothing," said Sham. But he let me tell the kid to wait there because we had to go around the corner to get something. We said we'd give him another fiver when we came back if he was still there.

"We may be a long time," warned Sham.

Then we went around the corner and legged it. We went three streets away and when we stopped we started laughing at the thought of that kid waiting for another fiver to come around the corner. That was so funny! We cracked right up and laughed and laughed till it hurt. And all the rest of the night, all one of us had to say was—"Do you think he's still there?"—and we'd crack up laughing all over again.

We'd spent more money and we still had nothing. We carried on just walking. At last we spotted a little group of kids turning down an alleyway and we followed them. They led us to a street of derelict houses.

There were plenty of houses to choose from. There must have been a lot of people hidden away in there.

We found ourselves a room on the second floor of a house with no staircase. Sham said if anyone came they'd have a hard job climbing up to us, while we could get away over the roofs or down a drainpipe at the back.

It was cold and damp. We pulled some wallpaper off the walls to cover ourselves and we even found some old clothes stuffed in a damp cupboard. Sleeping wasn't easy even when you forgot about the cold and the hard boards and began to doze. First some drunks came and talked and shouted for hours before they went to sleep down below. Later on still we heard kids screaming. It was just a couple houses down. "They're coming! They're coming, they're here!" someone was yelling. Other kids started up, then—some screaming and others shouting at them to shut up.

Someone yelled, "Squads!" There was panic then! Kids were running. I was going to run but Sham grabbed me.

"They won't look up here for us if they get enough down there," he hissed. We hid but no men came. Later on, from the arguments going on, it sounded as if someone'd had a nightmare. A few hours later the whole thing happened again but now we knew what was going on and we just lay and listened to make sure it was okay.

I was aching and still tired when we woke up. It was dark but I could hear people moving about. When the early light came we crept down. There were the drunk men, four of them, all asleep. The place stank of booze and piss. Other kids were emerging at the same time, rubbing their eyes and picking their way over the rubble and rotten timber. We watched each other warily but no one spoke. There was a family sitting around a fire outside; a boy was breaking up wood and the man was cooking something that smelled good. He stared briefly at us, and then forgot us.

Sham and I stepped out of the broken-up street and back into the town.

"I wonder if she made it?" said Sham.

eleven

Luke's was a really stupid place to meet. People knew us. You can bet every shopkeeper and especially Luke had been asked about Sly Sham and Fly Pie Shelly. Mother's Big Boys would be looking out. Maybe Shiner would be waiting around. And, of course, the Monroes. We had to get right into Coulsdon without being spotted. And then we had to get out again.

The number 26 bus goes nearest to Luke's shop. It stops opposite a little side road and we had to run for the passage with a bush growing out of the wall where Luke has his shop. We jumped out and ran like two rats in the gutter and we didn't stop till we got right into the shop.

I burst in first all out of breath. There was a woman buying bread rolls and she turned to glare at us. Luke made a terrible face at me when her back was turned. His eyes bulged and his mouth fell open. Luke's got a funny face, you can always tell exactly what he's thinking. When Sham barged in, his eyebrows nearly shot off his head. He managed to keep quiet until the woman had gone.

"Get outta my shop," he hissed. "What d'yer mean coming in here?"

"Please, Luke, just for an hour or so . . ." I began.

"An hour? An hour of hell with you two in my shop? One second is more than I can stand!" He stabbed his finger at me. "You're trouble! You've gone bad—don't argue! The people I've had in here asking for Fly Pie. It's been Fly Pie, Fly Pie, Fly Pie all week long and now here he is bringing trouble into my nice shop. Go on—scram!"

"We have to meet my sister here . . . we said . . ."

"Her too?" groaned Luke. There were footsteps; someone was walking up to the shop. He put his hands to his head and grabbed hold of the two big gray tufts of hair he has growing above his ears. "Go on, quick, round the back . . ." He reached over the counter and almost threw us behind him into the bakery. "You get spotted here and what'll I do? What'll happen to me? Trouble—scram—go on!"

We ran round the back. We heard Luke trying to put on his best shop manner but anyone who knew him could tell he was in a state. Luke was just no good at this sort of thing. When I peeped through at him he was glancing all the time over at us.

We were surrounded by pies and bread rolls and pasties and pastries and the smell was gorgeous. We were both dribbling. My stomach felt as if it was kicking me from inside, I wanted so much to eat. I saw Sham's hand steal out to try some warm little bread sticks but I slapped out at it.

"Don't steal from your own," I said.

Sham just groaned. I didn't blame him.

Luke came round the back as soon as the customer left. "What have you done?" he demanded. He waved his hand as I began to answer. "Don't tell me, do you think I want to know your troubles? Some friend you are." He stared at me, scowling fiercely. "Do you still want to be a baker?" he demanded.

"Yes," I said.

"Well you can't!" he yelled. "Bakers don't get into trouble. Bakers look after their shops and they bake bread and pastries and cakes and that's all they do. They don't get rich, they don't have people looking for them who can't find them and they don't go looking for trouble!"

"I didn't look for it, Luke," I begged. "It just . . . found me."

"Trouble isn't a lazy good-for-nothing," he said vehemently. "Trouble doesn't sit on its backside waiting for you to come calling. Trouble's not stupid—not like you," he observed. "Trouble goes shopping! Trouble's no baker. Trouble's a busy-body. Trouble knows tricks. And you fell for it!"

Just then another customer came and he had to dash out to serve them. But he was back in a minute, still rattling on—just like Luke.

"Trouble spotted you coming a mile off," he continued, as if he hadn't even broken off. He offered us each a chicken and ham pie as he spoke, and we bit into them—creamy, crispy and full of little nuggets of sweet chicken.

"Trouble said to itself—there's a boy who ain't going to end up being a baker—I'll see to that. That's what trouble said to itself when it saw you. And trouble was dead right!"

Then he had to dash out again to see another customer. Sham glanced at me.

"Does he always go on like that?" he asked through a mouthful of pie.

"When he's excited," I said. Then I thought about it and added, "Most of the time."

Next time he came back Luke had some apple turnovers.

"You don't deserve cakes," he said angrily. "You deserve to be stuck in a hole with stale bread rolls, you do." He watched us stuff the turnovers into our mouths—all crunchy with sugar and full of sweet apple. Luke's eyes bulged. "Don't stuff 'em, eat 'em," he raged. "Don't you even know how to eat?"

"Sorry," I mumbled. He always hated to see people stuff his food. But I could never help it.

"Well? What are they like?" he asked anxiously.

We both nodded. Everything Luke made was delicious.

"I'm too hot-blooded to make good pastry, I am," exclaimed Luke. "Too excitable. How someone like me manages to make pastry—or stay out of trouble—I just don't know. Now look at you—you've got hands cold as two spoons you have, you'd have made pastry like anything—and here you are, up to your neck in trouble and you'll probably never make so much as a cheese straw ever again for all I know!" He glared at me and flapped his apron so that the flour clouded up around him. "If only you hadn't got a dough head you'd have made something of yourself!" he snapped. "Trouble, you are—and in my shop!" He moaned, clutching his hair at the thought of it. Then he ran out again to serve someone.

The morning passed like that—with Luke rushing in and out to scold us and serve customers and then popping back in to give us another treat.

We were waiting again. All that waiting! The worst of it was that Luke might have known something from the radio or newspaper. I only had to ask but I didn't because he'd guess what was going on and that wasn't fair. I think he might have chucked us out if he'd know just how bad it really was.

"Shall I ask him?" I kept saying to Sham, and Sham shook his head and chewed his nails. And then in a minute he'd say, "Do you think you should ask him?" And I'd have to shake my head.

Then Luke came back and this time he had a smart-looking woman with him. I couldn't believe he was showing us to someone. Then the woman said, "Davey!" and she came to me.

Luke was saying, "What a girl! Look at her—you'd give her a job in a bank. Look!"

It was Jane all the time! She looked so different dressed like that I didn't believe it till she hugged me, all dirty like I was. She had good clothes, proper clothes, and her hair was done and everything was beautiful about her—just like the people who have everything.

"You did it!" screamed Sham. "You did it!"

Jane shook her head. "Not yet," she said. "I didn't dare. Sorry."

Sham stared glumly but I didn't care, I just squeezed her because I was so pleased to get her back. My sister. She could do anything!

"Can you scram now?" begged Luke.

"We made it out, Davey, and we're nearly there," Jane said. Then she turned to Sham. "I'm sorry about what I said that night," she said. "I don't know if you did it or not, now." She shrugged and smiled ruefully. "That's the best I can do."

"That's all right," said Sham. He was blushing furiously. "You came back, didn't you?"

"I came back," said Jane proudly. "And you came back, too." They smiled at each other. "Here—there's someone wants to see you," she told him. She ran out to the shop and came back with a stroller—a posh new stroller and Sy sitting in it, holding one of Luke's bread rolls. She had a bad cold and she was all snotted up but she was dressed like a doll in a smart pink suit. She was so pleased to see Sham, she started struggling to get out to him. Sham carefully undid her belt and took her out and she crawled all over him.

"Hello, baby, hello," said Sham. Sy rubbed her snotty face in his hair. He smiled proudly, shyly. Jane grinned.

"Do you like my disguise?" she asked, swirling around prettily.

"Ain't she perfect?" demanded Luke. "A proper little lady. You'd never know she came off the street, would you? Now," he added, jerking his thumb over his shoulder. "Scram!"

Jane took no notice. "I've got something for you two," she said. She had some shopping bags on the back of the stroller. "Clothes. Disguise. See? You're not going to be street kids when we walk out of here. You're going to be real children." She grinned. "It'll take me half an hour," she told Luke. She put down the bags and went over to the sink to run some water.

"It'll take days to make these two look like anything," muttered Luke. But he went to the front of the shop where he put his little radio on to cover up the noise, and he let her get on with it.

Jane had soap and scissors and started by washing us and cutting our hair. The water from our hair ran black three times! We kept staring at all that murky water going down the sink and it didn't seem possible that hair could have all that dirt hidden away in it. That took long enough. Then she got the clothes out. Those clothes! She had shoes, real sneakers, not brand-new but really good. She'd got my size right but Sham's were a bit small—somehow, he always looked smaller than he was. But he didn't care. We had jeans, almost new, and sweatshirts and good padded jackets and even clean socks. Sham didn't want to put his on because he said they made his toes feel funny.

"It's a disguise, it's supposed to feel funny, stupid," she said, and he did as he was told.

"I called Mr. Tallus again, to tell him I couldn't make it,"

Jane told us as she worked. "I spoke to her this time. She's a nice lady." Jane smiled. She was brushing Sham's hair and he was standing all tensed up, wincing every time she brushed. I was laughing because he looked as if he was being tortured. "She loves her baby so much," said Jane wistfully. "She was crying on the phone. She kept asking me to give Sy to the police but I told her we wanted to prove to her that we could do things right. It's important, you see?"

Sham nodded desperately. "Yes, please, yes please," he moaned.

"We're nearly there," said Jane. "We're nearly there!" She kept saying that. "When Mrs. Tallus sees us all dressed up proper and nice she'll know we've looked after Sy really well."

Sham wiped his nose on his cuff and Jane nearly knocked his block off with the hairbrush.

"Don't do that!" she screamed. "What's Mrs. Tallus going to say when she sees you all snotty on your sleeve?"

"Sorry," cried Sham, hiding behind his arm.

I was laughing but it was my turn next. The worst bit was having my face cleaned. I'd got something on it that was so tough she had to scrub and scrub to get it off. It left a red mark for days.

"I've done it right this time," she went on. "I didn't do it last night 'cause it wasn't right. I've got a room—a proper rented room. I paid the rent for two weeks! Mrs. Tallus is waiting for my next phone call, and we'll tell her to meet us outside on the pavement—so we can look out of our window and make sure everything's okay. See? Like you said, Davey, right?"

"Please don't hurt me," I begged.

"And when it's all clear we just walk out of our front door and give her back her baby! And she'll be so thankful because we did it right and we kept her baby from all the crooks who just wanted to make money out of her. Maybe she'll even come into our room and have a cup of tea or something with us. I expect she'll want to know what's happened, won't she?"

It took ages to get us ready. Jane was really fussy. But in the end, when she'd brushed our hair and wiped our noses, we looked in the mirror and Fly Pie and Sham had gone.

"Wow," said Sham. Even with his fat lip he looked like someone on TV. He touched his face as if he didn't believe it. "Wow," he said again. "It really is me—isn't it?"

I goggled.

"How about that?" smiled Jane. "How about that? Now you're worth something. Now you're worth whatever anyone cares to give you!"

Before we went Luke gave us a bag full of cheese rolls and doughnuts. I ran to him and flung my arms around him and squeezed him. I'd never done that before. I was happy. I believed that Jane could keep all her promises and that it was going to work. I was nearly crying because he was my friend and I was so proud that there had been someone to turn to when I wanted help.

He hugged me back, but he looked at me sorrowfully. "You'd have made a good baker," he scolded.

"I still will, Luke."

But he shook his head. "Not now. You're in big trouble."

"It'll work out."

"You know me," he said. "I've stayed in my little shop and I've not had no trouble—working trouble or not working trouble. It's all the same. Now I've done something for you, you do something for me, right?"

"Okay," I said, although I knew I wouldn't like it.

"When you go through that door, I don't want to see you

come through it again, ever—do you understand me?"

"Not for ever, Luke," I pleaded. "Just until the trouble's gone."

"It's the same thing, Davey!" he insisted. "Trouble like this never goes away. It won't stop now. No more favors. Okay?"

I nodded.

"That's how I've stayed here. You know that. You've no business bringing trouble to me."

"I promise, Luke." We went away and I never saw him again.

I thought I knew Jane, but she just kept on surprising me. Now she'd turned us into different people. People treated us differently just because we were dressed like that. Jane arranged to meet us at a bus stop in Peckham so we didn't have to travel together and Sham and I walked along to catch the bus like a pair of school kids. I even had a kid try to beg money off me. I gave him ten pence and he made an ugly face at it because it wasn't enough.

Jane told us to take care and behave like proper children and not a pair of noisy kids. We didn't do too badly, but Sham being Sham, he had to try it on. He stole an apple from a barrow on the street.

"This disguise business is worth remembering," he remarked, biting into it.

"You've got the wrong idea," I scolded. But he was right. You could do anything if you looked right. Who would ever think a smart boy like that would bother stealing apples?

Jane was there in Peckham like she'd promised. She hugged us as if she hadn't seen us for a week. Then she led us off to see the room.

"I'll have to smuggle you in, because it's only me and the baby supposed to be there," she told us. "And once you're in you'll have to stay in and keep your traps shut. We don't want to get caught now. We're nearly there!" She turned and grinned excitedly at us. "Nearly there," she repeated, and she hurried us along, clip-clopping in her smart black shoes, like a little mother with her family.

Sy went to sleep in the stroller. She had two thick green lines of snot running down her face and Jane kept stopping and wiping it, but it came back almost at once.

"It's a lovely room, you wait." Jane tossed her hair—her smart, hairdo hair. She was bright and happy and certain everything would be all right. Sham and me felt the same way. She'd done it, just like she said.

The rented room looked out on a road with trees scattered down it—a proper little road with shops and lampposts. We were above a grocery shop. It was a real place to live. She had the key to the front door and everything. We could have all gone in there and no one would have stopped us but she wanted to be sure that the people in the other rooms didn't know there were two boys with her so she went up first and we had to follow after—first Sham, then me.

I was frightened going in. I'd seen so many front doors but they weren't for me to open. I walked up the stairs, along a corridor smelling of cigars and disinfectant. There was an old door thick with dark paint; number six. I turned the handle and there it was.

I'd been in shops and other places but I don't think I'd been in a real room that was a place to live. Rooms belong to real people. This one belonged to us.

There was a bed in one corner. In another, a stove and a little table with a couple of wooden chairs. There was a sink with a plate drying on the draining board. There was an electric kettle. There was an armchair and a wardrobe and a chest of drawers and little ornaments—a vase, a picture of a field with horses. Everything you needed to be a proper person.

Sham was lying on the bed grinning at me.

"Cuppa tea?" said Jane.

We all started giggling. It was like a joke—us in a real place! Sy was sitting in the stroller whining, not like she used to do when she saw us having fun.

"Ssssh—someone'll hear," hissed Jane. She put Sy on her hip and started bustling about—emptying the teapot, putting milk from the fridge in the cups. Sy watched from her viewpoint on her hip, and Sham and me watched too. It was like seeing someone do things in a film. Jane did it all perfectly. She kept turning around and grinning at us.

"We'll have a nice cuppa tea and some cookies, and then I'll nip down and make that phone call," she said.

I wished she hadn't said that.

I was looking at the armchair. I'd seen armchairs on the dump and I thought this one looked out of place, sitting on the worn carpet with a little grubby lace thing over the back. I sat down in it, feeling the rough fabric with my fingers. I crossed my legs and tried to look as if I was used to armchairs. I looked around at all the things—the things we'd paid for. The lampshade, the curtains, the crockery in the half-open cupboard. The carpet was old. I've seen better carpets on the dump. There was a fireplace with a gas fire. Sham turned it on; it worked perfectly. So did all the lights and the stove. I found a lamp in a corner with a ship on its shade and I kept turning it on and off to see the ship jump to life on the dull plastic.

Jane nodded at the window. "Look out there," she said.

We could see right down the road opposite. There was a

café on the corner. Down our road there was a grocery and a butcher and a couple of other shops. People were walking up and down shopping, cars going past.

"See that lamppost on the corner?" asked Jane. "That's where I'll get her to wait. She'll do like I tell her." She nodded to us. It was a fact; the rich woman would do like Jane said. "We can watch out and see—make sure she's on her own, see she hasn't got the police or anything. See?"

Sham was by my side looking out, too. I glanced at him. "She's learning," I said.

Sham nodded and smiled crookedly. "So long as she doesn't learn too much," he said.

Jane giggled. "Smarter than you thought, aren't I?" she boasted. She leaned over to pour the hot water into the pot, put the lid back on and covered the whole thing with a little woolly coat. "There!" she exclaimed triumphantly. We all stared at the teapot, at the little wisp of steam oozing from the woolly coat. "There!" said Jane again.

It was all coming real.

Jane handed around cookies to eat with our tea. She made us sit at the table to eat them with the plates held under our chins in case any crumbs fell onto the carpet.

"Is this what people in houses do?" asked Sham.

"What do you think?" scoffed Jane. But even though we held the plates right up under our chins, somehow the crumbs got to the floor anyway and we had to vacuum. We nearly had a fight over who was to use the vacuum cleaner. It just sucked things up! Jane had been vacuuming away all day so she didn't have a right to have a go at all really. In the end we crumbled up a couple of cookies just to have a go.

"I don't see why you need plates at all when you've got one

of these things," said Sham, watching the crumbs vanish up the mouth of the machine. Jane laughed at him, but he had a point as far as I could see. It's easy to see why people like to stay clean if they have machines like that to play with. Sham and me wanted to crumble up the whole packet but Jane wasn't having it.

"I want to save 'em for Mrs. Tallus when she comes up to see how we've been living," she said. She spoke about Mrs. Tallus as if she was our aunt or something.

The only wrong thing was Sy. She was whining the whole time. I began to get cross about it. She'd been a good baby before. She used to wail sometimes but she always cheered up. Now she was just being miserable and spoiling everything.

"She's not well," said Jane. She tried to wipe the snot away again, but the baby didn't like it and twisted and turned and screamed louder than ever.

"Let's have a go," said Sham. But now that he'd been away from her she wasn't so keen. She clung to Jane and cried and cried. Jane had some dried baby food which we mixed up with hot water but she wouldn't eat it. In the end, we put her in the stroller and wheeled her around and around. She stopped yelling and closed her eyes.

Jane bent down to watch her. Sham stopped rocking her but she stirred and whined, so he started up again.

"I'm going out," whispered Jane. "I'll see if I can get something for her."

"And phone them," said Sham.

Jane made a face. "I can phone them later, can't I?" she begged.

Sham said, "We've been wasting too much time. We should have had it all sewn up by now."

"A few hours won't matter," said Jane. "I've had it. I

haven't had much sleep, it's doing me in. Eh, Sham?" She smiled at him.

Sham made a face, but he said, "Okay," and smiled back.

In the end Jane didn't make it to the phone the whole day. No one said anything. Jane kept going, "Oh, that poor woman, she must be worried sick. . . ." But she was just saying it. She brought some medicine, and after Sy drank it she slept for hours. Me and Sham were dead beat too and we had a quarrel over who was to sleep in the bed. In the end we both did, top to tail. As soon as I lay down I felt so tired I wondered how I'd ever moved. The last thing I saw was Jane sitting by the table next to the window, looking out.

She was still there when I woke up. I'd been asleep for ages so I can't think she was there the whole time. I opened my eyes and watched her—her hair neatly brushed, her clothes clean just like she liked them. Her lips were moving. Then she picked up a tissue to her eyes and I realized she was crying.

It was embarrassing, but I was curious. She was getting it her way. What had she got to cry about? I slid off the bed and crept nearer to hear what she was saying. I got right up next to her, but I couldn't hear. Then she looked around and saw me. She jumped when she saw me standing so close.

"What's up?" I said.

She looked at me, all wet-eyed. "I'm so scared, Davey, I've been so scared . . ." she began. Then she looked all choked up and started crying.

I couldn't believe it. I never thought she was feeling like that. She seemed so sure of herself.

She started blubbing. "I've been praying, Davey. I've been praying all the time for God to make it work, but I don't know if He's going to let it happen. . . ."

I was terrified, then. "Don't talk like that, don't talk like that," I said. I glanced over at Sham, because I thought if he heard her talk like that he'd stop believing, too. What did she need God for? Either it was going to work or it wasn't.

"You don't know what it's been like on my own," she blubbed.

"Don't go on, Sham'll hear," I hissed. I'd have done anything to stop her going on like that. I stood and watched helplessly for a bit, then I said, "I'll make a cuppa tea, shall I?"

"Yeah, go on then," she said. She didn't smile. She blew her nose. She was a right mess, all snot and tears.

I went to put the kettle on and do those things I'd seen her do. I wish I could have helped her but at the time it was important that she had it all under control. Maybe it'd have been better if there'd been another girl there for her. When I looked back a moment later she was staring out of the window and holding her face as if something was hurting her. Then Sham began to wake up and she pulled herself together and went to make the bed.

Things got better after that. Sy woke up and she looked a lot better after that long sleep. Then we watched some TV. I'd only seen TV in a TV stand before, but now we had one all to ourselves. We watched for ages, but there wasn't anything on that was any good except one thing—the news. We were waiting all the time for the news—it was like seeing yourself on TV, almost. The funny thing was, so much had happened we'd stopped thinking about what Tallus had said on the phone that time so it took us completely by surprise when we heard it. I mean about the reward. The newscaster was going on about the kidnapped baby and we were all smirking one moment and then feeling scared the next, when he said, "A reward of three million pounds has been offered for any information . . ."

We didn't hear any more. We all jumped up, roaring, "Wa-ah!" We screamed—it was like a goal in the last minute of a big match! I expect we could be heard streets away. Sham yelled, "Yeah!" and punched the air and Jane just held her face and screamed and I just ran at the TV and started kissing it. Three million! We were millionaires! The money was ours already!

After that Sham wanted Jane to go and phone them right away in case they changed their minds, but it was late by that time and she didn't want to. I was terrified it might all go away too but Jane was in charge and she got her way. Sham grumbled a bit. But after all, she was the one who'd got us the money. I guess she was worn out and didn't have it left in her to put herself through the mill again so soon. After that we just sat looking at each other and grinning. I never felt so good as when I thought I was worth a million.

Sham was funny after that. He didn't know how to behave to Jane at all. Sometimes, if she gave him a drink or did something for him, or even just said something to him, he looked so pleased! But other times I caught him looking at her as if she was going to turn into something dreadful and fly away.

After we'd eaten dinner we gave the baby a bath. Jane had bought some special clothes for giving her back in, and we tried them on and she looked so nice, we were proud. It was just like Jane said. We'd looked after her, she was like our little baby sister. Now she was nice and clean and pretty like she'd been in the photographs. She was happy and it was all because of us. Jane scared Sham by saying she didn't want to give her back any more, she was so sweet.

"No, no . . ." began Sham, all panicky. Then he saw her face and smiled at his own foolishness and Jane was as pleased as Punch at being able to tease Sly Sham.

twelve

Jane had spent the previous night in the bed so Sham and I got another turn on it that night. It was Heaven!—the best night's sleep I ever had, even with Sham in there with me. I can understand why people sleep late in the mornings when they have beds like that—and I can understand why Mother never let us have them, even though we could have got them from the Tip without spending a penny. When the morning came Sham and I stayed in bed with the baby while Jane went out to get some milk and stuff.

When she came back, she said, "I called. She's coming today at twelve o'clock."

"What's the time now?" asked Sham.

"Nine."

We looked at each other. I've never woken up so fast.

"It's too quick," said Sham.

"We don't want to wait," said Jane.

"We haven't thought—we haven't made plans what to do."

"Well, we better make 'em. Listen—it's no good waiting

any longer," Jane said. "I've had enough hanging around. Get it over with."

Sham looked at me, his face white. It was all dreadful. Suddenly dreadful. He made a funny little noise. I stared out of the window at the lamppost where Mrs. Tallus would appear.

"Nearly there," said Jane. "This afternoon we'll all be millionaires."

It got very bad in that room. We were sick with fear. I never want to feel like that again. Jane was the worst. She was walking around in circles and then she had to go and lie down on the bed because she felt so sick. Sham sat at the table and lay his head on his arms as if he'd gone to sleep. I tried thinking about that three million but nothing made it any better.

"I'm gonna be sick," Jane groaned. She jumped up and got to the sink just in time. She was really sick. It sounded horrible.

"I'm going out," said Sham suddenly. I jumped up when he said that, because I realized I wanted nothing in all the world more than to get out of there.

Jane was drinking a glass of water. "If you go, you're not coming back," she snapped, spilling water down her chin. "You can't keep running in and out."

"Okay," said Sham. He made for the door and I followed right behind him.

Jane said, "Don't go." I stopped. "I can't stay here on my own," she pleaded.

I groaned, but I walked back. She was right—it wasn't fair. "You go if you want," I told Sham.

"I'll stay," he said. He walked back and sat back down at the table with his head on his arms, just like before. Jane wrapped her arms around her stomach and started walking up and down again. I stood by the side of the window, peering out at the road. It was busy out there. A group of people walked into the café. A couple of women were studying the fruit on the pavement down the road. A man paused to let his dog sniff the pavement. Normal London.

We didn't have a clock in there, but it seemed to me those three hours went by half a dozen times. Sy woke up and started whining again. Jane tried to make her swallow some more medicine, but she wouldn't take it and it kept spilling down her front.

"It's good for you, bloody hell," shouted Jane suddenly. Sy stared at her and began to scream. "It's her only decent top," muttered Jane, dabbing at the baby's front. "I can't go out and get another one, look at it . . ."

Sy was screaming her head off.

"What's wrong with her?" demanded Sham furiously, lifting his head.

"She's ill, I told you. She's got a temperature," said Jane.

Sham stared at her. "We can't give her back like that, ill," he said. "You told her we'd looked after her properly."

"I can't help it if I had to spend a night out, can I?" snapped Jane. "What do you want me to do—go and cancel it again? Go and get another room? What?"

Sham stared at her a moment and then laid his head back down on his arm. I felt worse than ever. I went to lie on the bed. Jane started walking up and down, talking in a little voice to the baby.

"I'm sorry, I didn't mean to shout," she murmured. "Soon it's going to be all over and you'll be back home with your mummy and your daddy. And Sham and Jane and Davey'll come and visit you, would you like that, Sylvie? And we'll bring you sweets and sing to you . . ."

Sylvie wailed louder than ever.

"Your mummy's coming as fast as she can. Do be nice and sweet so you can see your mummy, darling, and so your mummy knows you've been happy and had a good time," said Jane. "Look, she's going to come along just there . . . Look," she said, "there she is."

Sham and I jumped up. We ran and hid behind the curtains and looked out.

A tall woman in a long coat was standing under the lamppost on the corner opposite. She had blond curly hair and she was dressed in a certain way so you knew she was someone. She had that coat and gloves and she stood and looked so you knew it was her. Around her, the people hurried by, dressed in jeans and anoraks and old clothes.

"We shouldn't have asked her here," said Jane. "She's in the wrong place."

That's what a rich woman looked like whose baby was worth seventeen million pounds. We had her baby.

"Go on then," said Sham.

"You're coming. We're all going," insisted Jane.

I closed my eyes. "I can't," I said. "Maybe it's not her," I said suddenly, full of hope. We all stared back down at the woman.

"It's her all right," said Sham.

"She's a nice woman, isn't she?" Jane begged. But I couldn't tell.

All around the street the busy people went past. The fruit shop down the road, with boxes of fruit and vegetables out on the pavement. The café opposite. We could see the shadowy shapes of people sitting in there. Under our window the grocer's door tinkled faintly as someone came out. Cars drove past.

A cyclist. A group of women with bags on their arms paused at the fruit shop and a tall man with a turban and a beard walked swiftly past not looking at anyone. Mrs. Tallus glanced at her watch and peered like a nervous bird, this way, that way, up and down the street.

"Come on, then," said Jane.

The rich woman stopped moving and stared. Across from her on our side of the road a girl was rattling a stroller across the uneven pavement. She was a few doors down the road from us. She had a boy about our age with her. She saw the woman looking so intently at her, and looked back and smiled uncertainly. Mrs. Tallus stared hard. The girl paused. She must have thought she was being summoned. She turned the stroller to face her and glanced up the road at the traffic to cross over.

Mrs. Tallus screamed. Her pretty face. She pointed and screamed and the whole street changed.

The women dropped their bags and ran at that girl with the stroller. The man walking by turned and ran at her too. People came running, out of shops, out of doors, jumping off bicycles and out of cars. The doors to the café burst open. Everywhere people were running. It was as if it had never been a street at all and everyone was just pretending.

The girl took a couple of steps back before the women got her. They grabbed her arms. The man got the boy and pushed him into the wall. Other women began to wrench the baby from its stroller. It was screaming for its mother, but they opened the straps and carried it away. The men began beating the girl. Mrs. Tallus had disappeared behind a wall of people and they carried the baby to her. The girl went down to the ground and they were kicking, hard. Everything was quick, sudden. Everything focused on Mrs. Tallus and her wall of big men and that little baby.

We saw glimpses behind those men. She was holding the baby up to her face—the screaming, twisting baby. She stared and saw . . .

"It's not mine!" she screamed. We could hear her, right across the road, right across the crowds and screaming street. She screamed in a hoarse voice and threw the baby away. I saw her do it; we all did. One of the men half turned and put out a hand to catch it as if it was a ball, but he fumbled and the baby disappeared among the heavy feet dancing around the rich woman.

Sham screamed when he saw that. Jane slapped her hand over his mouth. Down below the men were still beating up the girl; it just went on and on. They'd started on the boy too, now. She kept trying to get across the road to her baby who had disappeared on the pavement but they weren't letting her.

"It's us, it's us," hissed Jane. Everything was falling apart. People running everywhere, in and out of shops and buildings. Mrs. Tallus was screaming and yelling and she was so ugly and full of rage. I thought those men would pull the place down. The men were everywhere. They had guns. They found another baby and brought that one to her, but she slapped it out of the way. Everyone was screaming.

Jane pulled away from the window. They were kicking down doors. Sham was staring at her and his face was like Mrs. Tallus's face.

"You promised," he screamed. "You promised!"

"Shut up," hissed Jane. She tried to push him away but he grabbed her. I thought he was going to smack her one and I nearly went to stop him, but he was pushing and shoving her to the door.

"You get down there—you go down, you tell her, you tell

her," he was yelling. He was dragging her. Jane pulled away, holding the baby in one arm while he pulled the other. Sy was screaming and yelling.

"I don't want to, I don't want to!" Jane screamed.

"You go—you go and give her back her baby. That's what you're here for. You bloody promised!" He was so mad, he was almost hitting her. He grabbed hold of her top and flung her so hard it ripped.

"Go on, go on!" I screamed. I joined in, I started pulling at her, too. He was right. It was her job!

"Don't make me go, Davey, they'll kill me," wailed Jane. But we weren't missing our chance. We were too strong for her. Sham had one arm and I was behind pushing. She was crying and screaming.

"Leave the baby here," I said suddenly. "Just talk to her, see?"

We all stopped suddenly. Jane looked at the window. You could hear screams and men shouting.

"I said I'd bring her her baby . . ." she whimpered.

We started on her again and got the baby off her and bundled her out of the door. Outside, in the hall she realized it was useless to fight us and got her courage back. "All right, then! All right!" We stopped. "I'll tell her, right?"

Downstairs someone kicked the house door. It was violent, so violent the whole house shuddered. Jane looked at me for a second. Then she ran downstairs.

Sham and I ran back and hid behind the curtain to watch. Sham had his hand over Sy's mouth to stop her squealing. The street was emptying fast, except for that woman and her thugs. The shopkeepers were putting down their shutters, people were running to get away. The thugs were smashing up shops and banging in and out of the houses, but they couldn't get into ours. They'd finished with that girl. She was crawling across the road for her baby. One of the men had picked it up and he handed it to her, and I don't think it was too badly hurt. All around Mrs. Tallus was a thick wall of people, looking this way and that, moving fast, looking dangerous. Then Jane stepped out onto the street.

Somewhere there was a siren. Next to her was the boy they'd beaten up, lying on the ground by the wall, covered in blood. Jane stopped and looked at him for a second.

"Get on with it," hissed Sham.

She ran across the road. She reached up and pulled at a man's sleeve. I couldn't look. They'd murder her! She was so tiny. The man wrenched his sleeve away. She tried again. He flung out his arm and swatted her. She flew onto her back in the middle of the road. We lost sight of her, but she was back up in a minute, edging around the crowd, looking for a way in.

The thugs were scared, too. The siren was getting close. Jane tried again. I could see her mouth opening and shutting. Then a car came—a great black thing, screeching around the corner. It was going so fast I thought it was going to hit someone, but they scattered and it pulled up by the circle of thugs. Now the car was in between Jane and Mrs. Tallus. We saw the wall of men open and the lady stooped to get inside. Jane was knocking on the glass, but the car jerked and shot off. All around her men and women ran, bodyguards and thugs and agents, running so hard that in a minute the street was empty, suddenly empty. Jane was almost on her own out there.

She turned to look at our window: we stared back from our safe place. The police siren was very close now. Jane ran back to the house.

thirteen

There was blue light flashing. We lay on the floor out of sight. At last Jane got up and drew the curtains and sat down on the bed. Sham got up and sat at the table with his fists clenched at the sides of his head. He didn't move a muscle when Jane started weeping. I didn't go to her, either. She deserved it—she deserved all she got. Like Sham said, she'd promised. You shouldn't make promises you can't keep, not that sort of promise. She'd had it all her way. She'd made me lose Luke, she'd made me give back that money that could have bought me out. Now I was another kid on the street with nothing. I just watched her cry and I thought she had it coming to her, and I waited to see what she would do next.

It was very quiet in that room, except for Jane crying. Sy knew that if she screamed she'd get a hand clapped over her mouth so she just crouched on the floor and whimpered. As far as she was concerned she was back where she'd started when we found her with that tape over her mouth. We'd turned into people like the men who took her. She was waiting too, to see what was going to happen.

After a long time Jane went to the sink and washed her face. She touched carefully the swollen side of her face where that thug had hit her. Then she got her bag, the little black bag that was part of her posh new outfit, and started doing her makeup.

"We're going to get out," she said, sniffing away her tears and rubbing something on her cheek. She glanced in the mirror at Sham with his hard, still face, at me curled up in the armchair. "This place is dangerous. They'll search. The police. They'll do a better job than her thugs. Her thugs," she repeated viciously.

She was brushing her brown hair now, glancing every now and then at us. "We'll get out, right out this time—out of London to some place where we can get ourselves settled in. Somewhere they won't be looking for us. Somewhere to stay before we try again," she added, glancing at us in the mirror.

Sitting at the table, Sham bared his teeth and twisted up his face as if it hurt him to hear her saying that. He didn't say anything, just screwed up his eyes and face like that. Jane watched him and then started on her hair again.

"The train," she said. "That's the quickest. We'll catch a train out, way out. We can talk once we get away. All right?" she asked, looking at Sham again. He shook his head slowly.

"All right, Davey?" she begged.

I shrugged. "All right," I said.

Now Jane was tidying up, getting the bottle, the baby things. She was talking all the time as if she could convince herself and us that the terrible thing hadn't happened, that her plan was still on the rails. Sham stayed at the table with his head between his fists. I could see his eyes staring at the table.

When she had everything ready she said, "I'll go first. I'll meet you at Waterloo Station. Okay? We'll get a train. . . ."

"We get the ransom," said Sham slowly. He and Jane looked at each other. "You mucked it up," he said. "You don't keep your promises. Now we get everything—the whole seventeen million. She don't deserve a baby, that woman. You saw what she did. You saw how she threw that other baby. You saw what they did to that girl." He was shouting now. "She doesn't deserve nothing," he yelled.

He was shaking with rage and he was nearly crying. You couldn't tell who he hated most—my sister for letting him down or that woman for not loving babies like he thought she should.

"She can pay," he cried. "She pays for everything. She can pay for her baby."

"Stop shouting," hissed Jane. "You want to get us caught? We can talk about it later," she said.

"We don't need to talk," said Sham. "You mucked it up."

"You didn't do it my way," hissed Jane. "You gave us away— we know that, we're not stupid, are we, Davey? You tried to sell us to the Monroes. If it wasn't for that old man . . ."

"I did it your way," he screamed.

"I made you, I made you, that's why," Jane screamed back. "Now you make me do it your way. Try!"

"You won't make me—you won't make me do anything, never again!" challenged Sham. They were yelling their heads off. They'd forgotten everything. Sy was crying again but they didn't seem to care.

"Shut up, shut up," I shouted. "What are you doing?" I begged Jane.

She glared at me. "All right," she said. She was shaking too.

"Listen—we get out first. Then we talk about it."

Sham shook his head. "No talking. Can't you see?" He was begging her to understand now. "Look—we have to get her to leave us something. Then we pick it up," he explained. "Then we leave the baby and then we tell her where to find her. It's the only way, because if we ever meet her she'll kill us. We can't ever meet her. Can we, Fly?" he begged me.

Sham was right. She didn't want to be given anything, not even her baby.

"He's right," I said. "We can't ever meet her."

Jane looked defiantly at me. "You used to say we could never trust Sham, either," she said. Then she looked away from me. "I don't want nothing of hers anyway," she muttered.

There was a window at the back of the house leading out into a narrow alley where the shops dumped their rubbish. Jane slid out and I handed her the baby and the stroller.

She looked up at me. "See you in Waterloo." She tried to smile.

"Leave the baby," I said.

Jane winced.

"Leave her there in the stroller," I said, pointing to a gap between two boxes. "Leave her for Sham or anyone. It didn't work," I said.

Sy was on her hip watching me. She seemed to understand something of what I was saying because she clung to Jane and cried.

Jane shook her head. "Not yet, Davey," she said. "She's all we got."

She picked her way past the black garbage bags, the piles of litter, the cardboard boxes and heaps of yellow cabbage leaves and disappeared around the corner into the back streets.

* * *

the baby and fly pie
165

We'd been lucky. That's how I looked at it. We'd been lucky to clobber Shiner, lucky to escape the Monroes in Santy, we'd been lucky not to get picked up on the street by the police or the Death Squads and we were lucky again to get away from Mrs. Tallus's thugs. We were still lucky, in a way. There were a lot of police about but they took no notice of two smart boys waiting for the bus. I didn't think the same would be true of Jane.

On the way I tried to convince Sham that it was time to pack it in. But Sham clenched his teeth and screwed up his eyes like he'd done in the room—as if it hurt to talk about it. I knew what was going around his mind: seventeen million quid.

I gave it up and stared out of the bus window. I thought of the little room we were leaving behind—the plates still drying on the draining board, the packet of cookies we'd forgotten in the cupboard, the vacuum cleaner, the little ornaments on the windowsill and the sideboard, the bed with a real mattress. Jane had been so proud of it. It was all she ever wanted but it was gone forever.

She was there at the station waiting for us. I was surprised and disappointed—surprised because she'd got through, and disappointed because if they'd picked her up I'd be free.

She watched us anxiously as we came through the ticket hall toward her. She was sitting on a bench and Sy was pottering about, holding herself up on it. She kept clinging to Jane's knees and whimpering and looking up at her. Jane stood up when she saw us coming, smoothed her skirt over her legs and sat down again.

She started up again as soon as we got there. How that woman couldn't be blamed because she was scared for her baby. How it was her baby after all and she was entitled to do what she wanted to get her back. How now that she knew we were too clever, we could meet her again, and that once she saw us and talked to us it'd be different. She whined on and on . . .

Sham blew up. Right there in the middle of the ticket hall with all those people wandering about he blew up.

"You shut up," he yelled. "We had everything. All that money, but you mucked it up because you're too bloody good for it—too good to take anything and you stopped me taking mine. You've got to understand, you're wrong, you're wrong!" He was screaming. He didn't even seem to be aware that there were people walking past staring. He just wanted her to admit that she was wrong and he didn't care if the whole world heard.

I shoved him roughly. "Shut up," I hissed. "You want to get us killed?"

He turned to glare at me. His eyes flickered over the thick crowds hurrying around us. "Tell her to shut up, then," he growled. "I don't have to listen to her."

Jane's mouth opened again. She had nothing left to give away. But she couldn't leave it alone—as if words could change anything.

"Not here," I begged. "Somewhere, but not here." She looked resentfully at me and nodded.

"Somewhere else," she agreed. She looked at Sham as if she could change him into another person. "I'll get the tickets," she said.

And our luck still held. There were police in the station, we'd been arguing in public like that, but Jane got the tickets and we walked past the ticket man and onto the platform and onto the train and no one stopped us. It was like a miracle to me because I was sure they were looking for us. We seemed to be invisible.

None of us had ever been in a train before. Jane folded up

the stroller and put it on the rack above us and we sat in a row and waited. Sy was whining away the whole time, she hadn't stopped whining all that time. I could see people watching us curiously but there was nothing we could do about that.

"Is your baby all right?" asked an elderly woman across from us.

Jane glared at her. "We're just taking her home," she said crossly, tossing her hair. The woman made a face and turned away.

Jane gave Sy a bottle and offered her to Sham to hold, but he made an impatient gesture. Sy closed her eyes firmly, as if she could make us and her whole life this past week go away by not looking, and she sucked as if it would save her life.

The train stood at the station for ages. We were sweating, but when it pulled away I was suddenly happy. We were leaving everything behind us. I felt that all the problems in the world were left back there on the station. It was so nice—the speed of the train, the way it rattled smoothly along. We all felt the same.

"We done it—we got away again," Jane whispered in my ear. I smiled at her and even Sham looked up from the window and smiled. It felt so good to be rattling away from London, the streets, the gangs, Tallus, the Monroes, the police. The train got going and it settled down into a steady rattle and roll. People got out newspapers or books or looked out of the window. Sy fell asleep. I was exhausted. I leaned back and closed my eyes and let the train rock me. There was a little sunlight shining across my arms and neck and it felt so warm and nice. . . .

I must have dozed. We'd stopped. People got on and off. I didn't know where we were going—just away. We waited anxiously until the train started off again. I tried to doze again because it had been so nice. I was still trying when Sham leaned forward and whispered to Jane.

"How much money's left?"

She made a face. "About twenty-five," she said.

I opened my eyes and stared at her. It wasn't possible. . . .

"The room—I had to rent it for two weeks, you can't rent a room for a day," she whispered, glancing nervously at the people on the seats near us. "You have to pay an advance and a deposit. And those clothes . . ."

All that money. Over a thousand pounds—gone.

"Here . . ." Jane dug in her bag and handed Sham a little black purse. "You look after it now."

Sham waved it away in disgust. Once, there'd been seventeen million pounds. Twenty-five quid wasn't worth bothering with. We'd have sold each other for twenty-five quid a few days ago.

He turned away but a little later he said, "Go on then. The way you spend it . . ." She handed it over to him and looked as if she was about to say something. But she changed her mind and glanced at me instead.

I closed my eyes and tried to let the warm sun, the rocking train and the clitter-clatter-clitter-clatter of the rails lull me back to sleep.

A few more stations came and went. I tried hard but I couldn't sleep. The evening sunshine died and it was growing dark outside and cold in the train. We pulled up into another station—a big one.

"I'm hungry," I said. I hadn't had anything to eat all day. I hadn't been able to manage breakfast. Jane rummaged in her bag and took out the paper bag Luke had given us only the day before. Doughnuts, cheese rolls. We started stuffing—even

Jane. At one point I looked up and people were staring at us because we were eating in a way no good clean children wearing the sort of clothes we had on ever eat. Jane nudged us and whispered, "Eat it nicely. . . ." She tried to smile at one of the women who was watching.

"Just a joke," she said thickly, through a great chewed wad of bread and cheese. The woman closed her eyes tiredly and looked away.

Sham peered out among the hurrying people. There was a kiosk selling drinks and snacks on the platform just along from us. "We need something to drink," he said. "Can of Coke or something . . ."

"There's no time, is there?" said Jane.

A man on the other side of the corridor looked across. "You've plenty of time," he said. "They stop here to take off some coaches." As he spoke the train jolted. He smiled. "There," he said.

"Go on, then," said Jane, nudging Sham with her elbow. "Couple of cans of something. Get some juice for Sy."

Sham jumped up. I saw him a few seconds later in the line at the kiosk watching the train anxiously.

I'd bolted my bread roll. I felt a buzzing in the back of my head. I was so tired but I wasn't sleepy. I looked at Jane and she stared back at me, just looking. I don't know what she was thinking; she was beyond me most of the time. I glanced back out. Sham was being served.

I looked away—at the man reading his paper, at the people in the seats around us sunk in their own thoughts. Then I looked out of the window again.

Sham was gone.

I nudged Jane and pointed.

"Maybe they didn't sell what he wanted," she muttered.

She sat and chewed at her fingers for a bit, then she leant across and asked the man opposite, "How long before we go?"

The man glanced at his watch. "A couple of minutes," he said.

She nudged me. "Go and have a look—he might think he's got more time than he has."

Outside on the platform it smelled of dirt and metal. There were people running, walking, some sitting. A man in uniform had started walking down the train slamming the doors. Sham was nowhere to be seen. I walked toward the kiosk, since that was the last place I'd seen him. Beyond the kiosk a man was selling newspapers. There was one of those triangular stands with the headlines on it, and on the front of it was a drawing of Jane's face.

I stared like an idiot. She was staring out of the paper at everyone. It was just a drawing but it was good. For a second I couldn't tear myself away, then I looked about out of the corner of my eye to see if anyone had noticed me. I felt I was in a spotlight. I glanced up at the man selling papers. He was shouting something, but you couldn't understand a word of it. He had a paper in his hand and there was a big pile of them at his feet. On the front page were three faces—Jane, Sham and me.

I ran back to the train. I sat down and begged it to go. I looked desperately at Jane.

"Didn't you see him?" she asked.

I shook my head. "He's gone," I mouthed. I didn't blame Sham. It was all up. The whole country was looking for us. Our faces were in the papers, on TV. The only thing was to get rid of the baby—fast. I stared at Jane trying to make her see, because we were surrounded by people and I couldn't say.

the baby and fly pie
171

Jane stared back. Then she got up.

"Come on . . ." She was pulling the stroller down from the rack.

"Jane . . . !" It was terrible. Why couldn't I make her do anything, why wouldn't she trust me just this once?

"We're getting off. We can't leave Sham," she said flatly.

"Jane, please . . . please, Jane," I begged, but I despaired of ever making her see anything. The man with the paper was helping her down with the stroller.

"Lost your friend?" he asked sympathetically. "He's probably gone to the toilet—he'll be here." But the train was about to start. Someone was shouting on the station. "Perhaps not," he murmured, frowning. "But you can catch another in an hour," he added.

I shuffled past him, trying to hide my face. Jane brazened it out, smiling and laughing.

"He's always like that—no sense in him," she laughed. "We have to do this all the time!" We had to push out past people piling into the train at the last minute. Sy woke up and started to whimper. I was getting to hate that. She was crying by the time we got off. The man put the stroller down.

"Poor little thing," he said. "That lad wants telling what for." He smiled and shrugged and closed the door.

We were on the platform just yards from the pictures. I watched while Jane strapped Sy in and stuck a pacifier in her mouth. Sy spat it out and started to wail.

I grabbed Jane's arm and started pulling at her, getting her away from the paper man, away from the lights of the station. It was almost dark now and we had to get on the streets and away from the lights.

"What is it? What's the matter, Davey?" she asked irritably.

"Just come on," I said. At last she let me lead her. We got past the barriers. It was bright in the ticket hall. There was another news-seller.

Her face—her face, staring out at all those hundreds of people with the word "Kidnap" over it. Jane stopped suddenly, stared. She glanced at me, put her head down and we hurried out.

In the air outside, the smell of car exhausts and burgers. People were begging at the entrance—outstretched hands waiting for coins, for crusts, for half-eaten sandwiches or unfinished cans of lemonade or Coke that travelers kept for them. We pushed past onto the brightly lit tarmac outside.

On our left was a man leaning against the wall reading a newspaper; our faces watched us. We turned right and walked past a row of taxis, the drivers in the lit interiors watching us with expressionless faces as we trotted too fast past them and into the wonderful darkness under a poster on the wall. We followed the main road around, stuck on the pavement under a high gray stone wall. On the other side was the town, bright and gaudy with lights and people. There were no side roads, no quiet streets with poor lights to escape into; we felt trapped under that tall wall. Sy was talking to herself and crying in between, but she shut up when Jane shook the stroller angrily.

There was a traffic circle and at last a little road leading off it under a railway bridge. We followed it for a while but it ended at a factory gate. We found a footpath leading away into the dark fields and we followed it, pushing the stroller over the damp mud, splashing through puddles, fearing to meet someone in this suspicious place.

After a couple of miles we were walking by a broad river. The path petered out and we were in the dark of fields, stumbling in mud and muck and tripping over the rough grass. The going got rough and we had to carry the stroller between us.

It was cold and we had nothing to cover us. We'd done this over and over but every night we had nothing to cover us. After a very long time we saw some lights and we walked toward them, only for a direction. The river got in our way, though. We carried on along the bank until it curved around again—then we came to an old barn. Most of it was mud trodden deep by the cows, but in one corner was a heap of straw.

Sy didn't wake up when we lifted her out of her chair and covered her with straw. Then we made our nest and crept in.

As soon as we sat down Jane was off.

"I should have just gone out with her and given her to her and shown her," she wept. She was trying to wipe her nose with the hay. "Or we should have left her like you said, or given her to the police or the soup people or the church or something." She was really crying now. "It didn't work, none of it worked and I mucked up our chance, didn't I, Davey?" I couldn't say anything because it was true. I just hugged her.

It was dark, as dark as anywhere I've ever been. After a while, I could make out one or two little stars shining through holes in the roof. They were the brightest stars I'd ever seen. They kept coming and going under the clouds.

fourteen

Sy kept waking up in the night coughing. In the end Jane gave her a bottle of milk which she'd tucked down her blouse to keep warm.

"Poor little thing," she whispered as she crept back in the dark beside me. I kept waking up after that—watching the darkness pale and then get lighter.

It was quite light when something came in through the door—something enormous squelching in through the mud. I was scared for a second, but it was just a cow, a big black and white one. I'd never seen cows close up. It was huge. It almost jumped when it saw us. It sort of shuffled backward and watched us from halfway through the door. Then it backed up and went outside again.

Jane and the baby were still asleep. My sister was lying on her side with the light from the holed roof on her face. Her makeup was all over the place, smudged by tears. She had hay in her hair and she was a right mess. I thought how she'd helped me and brought me up when I was small, and how she was still trying to help me now, even though it had all gone so horribly wrong. I felt sorry for her then and I wanted to tell her—I wish I had, but I didn't want to wake her up. She couldn't have done more for me, no one could. She was a good person, she made things happen, but you can't change the whole world.

I wanted to do something for her and I remembered the cows. Cows meant milk. I could get some milk for her and the baby.

Outside it was a misty, cool morning. It smelled wonderful—of hay and wet grass and cows and the air was sweet. There was a film of wet spiderwebs over the whole field. The mist hung in blankets over the fields and hedges and the cows were walking through the wet grass, or pulling mouthfuls of it and puffing cloudy breath into the air. There was one standing nearby watching me. I held out my hand and walked slowly toward her, saying, "Come on, girl, come on," as if she were a dog.

The cow watched me and started backing off when I got close. I speeded up and so did she, and then she turned and ran off. I tried another one, and then another but I couldn't get near them. I don't suppose I'd have known how to get the milk out even if I had.

I walked around for a bit, wondering what to do. There were some mushrooms growing in the grass, but I didn't know if you could eat them or not. Then I found some blackberries growing on a hedge. I was so pleased. There were loads—I ate handfuls of them and then filled my pockets for Jane. I was still picking them when I heard Sy cry and I headed back to the barn.

Jane was lying in the hay with her eyes open, ignoring Sy,

gazing at the wall of the barn. I came in quietly in case she was praying again but her lips were still. Then she heard me and sat up.

"She wants a drink," she said. There was a bit of milk in the bottle left over from the night before, but Sy was just as keen on my blackberries as she was on milk. She loved them! She was opening her mouth wide and leaning forward going, "Ah, ah, ah!" and she couldn't take her eyes off them. She made us laugh. Jane ate some too.

"I'm sorry, Davey," she said.

I shrugged. It didn't matter now. I just wanted to get her out alive.

We finished the berries. "Do you want some more?" I asked. "There's loads more."

"Go on then, please," she said. So I went out and got some more, and that, with some of the doughnuts Luke gave us, was our breakfast.

A little while later we heard a tractor droning away in the fields outside. I ran out to have a look. I could see it, two or three fields away. It was coming in our direction.

Quickly we packed Sy up in the stroller, gave her a chunk of doughnut to keep her quiet and hurried out. We crouched low behind a brick wall and hurried out of sight.

We walked across the wet fields. We were walking no-where. We had to dump the stroller because it wouldn't go over fields. There was a wood ahead and we made for that. Inside it felt a lot safer and we sat down on some logs for a while, feeding Sy the last of the doughnuts. She sounded bad—coughing and rattling inside and crying all the time.

"We'd better get her some milk," said Jane. "And something for us. Then we can make another phone call."

I couldn't believe it when she said that. She was still trying but it was stupid now. I didn't say anything, though.

"Have you got any money left?" she asked me. I'd forgotten about that. I dug in my pocket and there was the fifteen pounds I had left over from the eighty she'd given me when we left Santy. I handed it over. Jane put it in her bag.

"We're still going, Davey," she said.

We stayed under the trees listening to the raindrops on the leaves a long way above our heads. When the weather cleared up, Jane said we had to get going.

Although it felt safer in the fields, where we could hide among the hedgerows, it was such hard work stumbling over the clumps of wet grass that when we found a little country lane, we stayed on it. There were plenty of thick hedges so we could usually get out of the way when a car came past. We walked on. The sun came through the clouds and warmed us. After a long time we passed a house; then another house. We were on the edges of a village or town.

The houses were very big, with large gardens. They stood back from the road, hidden away among the trees and hedges. I saw some trees with apples growing on them in one garden and I crept in and picked some while Jane watched out. They were sour but crisp and juicy. After that I thought I might be able to get into a house and steal some milk and food, but Jane wanted to go on to a shop. We argued about it on and off. We came to a house with a garden thick with overgrown shrubs and trees that was just right to raid, and we stood on the pavement outside peering in. Jane was chewing her lips and trying to convince herself.

"It's an emergency," she said, peering through the bushes. She thought it wasn't so bad stealing if it was an emergency. We walked up nearer the drive to get a better look.

Someone called behind us.

* * *

It was a woman. She had a couple of brown and white dogs on leads. We froze, but she was smiling, bustling up to us.

"You poor things, how on earth did you get into such a mess? You're both wet through! What on earth have you been doing?" she said. She was scolding us but she wasn't cross. We stood uncertainly as the dogs sniffed our legs. Sy cooed and waved her hand at them.

"And the baby—dear little thing. Did you get caught in the rain? But you're miles from anywhere!"

"We were looking for the bus . . ." began Jane, but the woman rattled on over her.

"You'll have to come in and get warm, I live just up there— no, no, no. I'd like a bit of company. My husband died, you see, I'm all alone—just me and Hip and Hop." She bent down and patted the two dogs. "They look after me," she said, smiling. Jane and I glanced at each other. But the woman was already hurrying us along down the road. We turned into a tarmac drive that curved around past bushes with shiny green leaves up to a big house with plants growing up the walls. There was a big blue car parked outside.

"Such weather we're having—wind and rain and sun and then all over again—it just can't seem to make up its mind, can it?" said the woman. She led us down the side of the house and opened a door with a key. We entered a long room with wooden cupboards all over the walls. There was a long dark table at one end and a sort of wide shelf with cupboards underneath along one wall. There was a stove and a kettle and all that sort of thing. On the wide shelf a radio was singing low.

"We can't stay long," said Jane. But she was perking up. The woman was friendly; everything seemed easy. "Me and my cousin were just out for a walk with my baby when the rain came," said Jane. "We're a bit lost. We went for a walk, see . . ."

"Now you sit down while I get a heater to warm you up and I'll put the kettle on. Do you drink tea? But I expect the young man will want chocolate and the baby will want milk—and some cookies of course—let me see . . ."

She was digging in a cupboard now, not waiting for an answer. "You should have known better than to go for a walk with no coats in this weather, but that's young people all over," she said, her voice muffled by the cupboard. Jane and I sat nervously down at the table. Jane took Sy on her lap. Sy cooed, looked anxiously at us. She found a shiny mat in front of her and she started to chew it and bang it. She began to shout at it. She coughed and rattled and looked at us and broke into a smile—the first smile in ages.

The woman came out and stood smiling at Sy. She was dressed in a loose gray coat and had gray hair and she looked plump and pink and very, very clean. She had an electric heater in her hand which she put on under the table so that a warm draft blew up around our legs.

"I hope you don't mind keeping me company for an hour or so," she said. She smiled again and went to the wide shelf and began cutting bread.

The woman quieted down a bit as we ate our toast. She fed the baby buttery scraps and warmed some milk for her. Jane began to talk—some invention about a few days away from London on the train and getting a place to stay in Reading and going for a walk and getting lost and catching the bus and on and on. The woman smiled and nodded and played with Sy.

As Jane talked I caught sight of myself in a mirror through an open door in the other room. I was a mess—covered in straw and hay, my face smeared with mud. Jane was sitting sipping her tea with her finger cocked like a little lady but her makeup was smudged all over her face. Her hairdo had collapsed with wet, she was daubed with dirt and mud and she looked nothing more than a little girl dressed up and drenched. The old woman didn't seem to notice. She seemed to think it was perfectly normal to find two kids with a sick baby out early in the morning, wet with dew and with hay in their hair.

"She must be a bit funny," I thought to myself. I was relaxed in the warmth of that heater, with the toast and hot chocolate inside me.

On the shiny surface over the cupboards the radio stopped playing music. In between Jane's words I heard a man say, "The news . . ."

The gray-haired woman got smoothly up and turned it off. "We don't want to listen to that," she said. She smiled and started bustling about, talking rapidly again—talking too much. I buried my nose in my drink and nibbled at my toast, but I wasn't hungry anymore.

It took the woman a while to calm down and stop talking so much. Then she said, "I'll just take my coat off and give the boys a drink." She got up and left the room with her dogs.

I said to Jane, "She knows."

Jane put her finger to her lips and shook her head disapprovingly.

I got up. Jane tried to stop me but I shook her off. The woman had closed the door behind her; I edged it open. She wasn't there. I went in and went up to another door and put my ear to it. I could hear her voice—low, urgent whispering.

I ran back. "She's on the phone," I said. "She's whispering on the phone. . . ."

There was a bolt on the door she'd gone out of and we put it to. Jane had Sy on her hip. I hissed: "Leave her!" She stared at me. "Please leave her," I begged. Jane nodded. She put Sy on the floor, bent and kissed her and then we ran out into the back garden and across the wet lawn. Sy screamed as we ran in between trees with apples and pears and plums growing on them. Behind us the woman was shouting but I think we ducked behind her shed before she saw which way we'd gone. Her voice was different now—angry, shrill, frightened. Then we were over the fence and running through the wet corn stubble behind her house.

"Down!" hissed Jane. We flung ourselves onto the hard stubble behind some bales of straw. After a time Jane peered up and she nodded. We quickly ran across the open space toward trees growing at the end of the field.

We pushed our way through wet green leaves and brambles that snatched at our legs and clothes and soaked us over again. We came to a rutted muddy track and stuck to that. Jane said, "Do you think they'll have dogs?" but apart from that we didn't speak. I remember very vividly the pale tree trunks, the green leaves turning yellow and brown and orange, the dark mud, the smell of wet earth and wet wood. A little later there was a siren back there.

We kept running. It was uphill all the way and we were terribly out of breath but we were doing all right. We'd stopped running, we were feeling safer, on our way. And then out of nowhere Jane sat down on a pile of stones at the side of the track.

"What are you doing?" I asked. I looked back. I thought I could hear cars racing on the roads, pulling up somewhere down the hill behind us.

She sat with her hands neatly folded in her lap. "I wish I'd brought her this far, Davey," she said. "I'd have liked to have given her to someone even if it was only the police."

"Don't be daft," I told her. "Come on." I pulled her arm.

She looked up at me with her white face. "Davey, I'm staying here."

There was a shocked second and then I grabbed her. I could have strangled her. I was saying, "Get up! Get up," and pulling and tugging. Every time it was obvious what to do she went right the other way!

She just said, "Don't, Davey, don't . . ." She sounded offended and I let go. "I'll tell them you went some other way," she said. "We split up, see? It's a chance. One of us'll get away. I'm going to stay here and tell them how it was. We're not what they think we are, see."

I licked my lips, like Sham. I glanced back down the path. They could come anytime. They could come now.

"Then it's not for nothing, if I tell them. Do you see? Here . . ." She got up and put her bag over my neck. "You get away, get to a town. Brush your hair, get all that straw and stuff out. Wash your face. You won't look half bad. You'll get away with it. Plenty of kids like you about."

She took her hairbrush out of the bag and brushed at my hair. "Like that." She nodded and put the brush back. "Like I did," she insisted.   ˙

I looked behind me. Everything was happening faster and faster. I'd promised myself I'd look out for her but when it came to it, all I wanted to do was save my skin.

Behind us were more sirens. Jane pulled a face. "They've got their precious baby back, haven't they, what more do they want?" she sniffed. "They don't need to bother with us. Pair of rubbish kids, we are . . ." She looked at me and made a face.

"You better get going. Don't worry about me. They'll lock me up. Plenty to eat and drink and all the rest and I'll talk and tell them what—you know me. They ought to know, didn't they? You run for it."

We hugged. Jane said, "We just wanted a life, didn't we, Davey?" Then I left her. She was sitting back down on that heap of stones with her hands in her lap when I ran off, looking back the way they'd come.

I ran up the track. Later I heard a car coming and I got off it just in time. I hid and saw it. It was unmarked. There were men in it, but no dogs. They had guns, though. They hadn't had time to get dogs but there were always guns.

I carried on up a little footpath. A couple of times I heard shouting but I left it behind. I carried on for ages, out of the woods and through scrubland, running all the time until I thought my heart would burst. It seemed to be uphill all the way but at last I pushed past some spiky green bushes and the hill fell away before me and there it was—a town. Houses spreading out for miles, tall office buildings in the distance. I knew I'd done it then, I'd got away, because every town is full of kids and we all look the same. No one was going to pick me out. No one would even notice one more lousy kid.

I waited just a minute to get my breath back and then I ran down, through the spiky bushes and the long gray grass. I'd gone maybe ten steps when I heard a gunshot. One shot, way off behind me. That's how they do it, through the temple or the back of your head. That's all they needed to do to shut her up forever. I almost fell over but only for a second. I didn't even think about it. I ran fast downhill and I felt like I was flying.

melvin burgess
184